ANGELS

The Inside Scoop on the Stars of

Charlie's Angels

by Nancy Krulik

Aladdin Paperbacks

New York London Toronto Sydney Singapore

First Aladdin Paperbacks edition November 2000
Copyright © 2000 by Nancy Krulik

Aladdin Paperbacks
An imprint of Simon & Schuster
Children's Publishing Division
1230 Avenue of the Americas
New York, NY 10020

Designed by Lisa E. Vega
The text for this book was set in Palatino
Printed and bound in the United States of America
10 9 8 7 6 5 4 3 2 1

Library of Congress Cataloging-in-Publication Data:
Krulik, Nancy
Angels : the inside scoop on the stars of *Charlie's Angels*
1st Aladdin Paperbacks ed.
p.   cm.
ISBN 0-689-84297-X
1. Drew Barrymore—Juvenile literature. 2. Cameron Diaz—Juvenile literature. 3. Lucy Liu, 1968– —Juvenile literature. [1. Charlie's angels (Motion picture : 2000)—Juvenile literature. 2. Actors—United States—Biography—Juvenile literature.]
PN2287.B29 K78 2000
[b] 00-062041
CIP AC

For Amanda,
who is growing up to be a truly powerful woman
—NEK

TABLE OF CONTENTS

LUCY LIU

INTRODUCTION

Charlie's Angels *Takes Flight*

Did you hear a bell ringing? You know what it means when a bell rings, don't you? Every time a bell rings an angel earns her wings.

One thing's for sure, getting *Charlie's Angels: The Movie* off the ground took a lot more than a pair of wings. The movie, which is loosely based on the hit 1970s TV show about three women crime fighters, certainly didn't have an easy start.

It was more than ten years ago when Aaron Spelling, creator of the original TV series, first tried to revive *Charlie's Angels*. Back then, Aaron planned to bring back *Charlie's Angels* as an all-new TV show. He'd even gone as far as to cast the show (a then-unknown Téa Leoni was slated to be one of the stars), but the networks weren't interested.

Aaron Spelling is one of the most powerful men in Hollywood. His hit series have included *Charlie's Angels*, *The Love Boat*, *Beverly Hills, 90210*, and *Charmed*. When he speaks, people listen. But even Aaron hadn't been able to get enough network interest to revive *Charlie's Angels*. Many people figured that if Aaron couldn't do it, no one could.

Never Underestimate The Power of A Woman.

In 1999, Hollywood actress Drew Barrymore went into negotiations to star in and coproduce a *Charlie's Angels* movie. The movie Drew imagined would be an updated view of women crime fighters—heavy on brains and comedy, but without the guns of the original TV series. As actor Sam Rockwell, who plays Drew's boyfriend in the movie, puts it, "These are not the same angels from the '70s. First of all, these angels don't have any guns. And also, they're super smart."

With Drew on board, *Charlie's Angels* suddenly became one of the hottest properties around. In recent years the young actress had developed a reputation for making feel-good films that brought in big crowds at the box office. Many actresses wanted to be associated with Drew. Eventually Cameron Diaz, the award-winning star of *There's Something About Mary*, signed on, giving

Charlie's Angels a double punch of woman power.

Finding an actress to play the third Angel in the film proved very difficult. It's not that there weren't a lot of actresses looking to play the part. Actresses were throwing their names and head shots into the ring even before the movie's producers had officially announced that they were looking for an Angel. "The amazing thing is we never issued one press release—ever," Leonard Goldberg, Drew's coproducer on the film, explains. "This had taken on a life of its own."

To be sure, there were plenty of great candidates for the third Angel spot. Everyone from Angelina Jolie to Lauryn Hill to Posh Spice was rumored to have been considered. But no matter what the producers did, they couldn't seem to find just the right actress— someone who was comfortable with martial arts, who had a strong sense of humor, and who could fix her schedule so it would coincide with the *Charlie's Angels* shoot dates.

Finally, after months of speculation—and one of the biggest star searches in recorded history—*Ally McBeal* actress Lucy Liu signed her name on the dotted line of the *Charlie's Angels* contract. Finally, the trio was complete. Those angelic bells could finally start ringing—and the cameras could start rolling.

Drew Barrymore. Cameron Diaz. Lucy Liu. Three of the hottest women in Hollywood are now starring together in one of the most highly anticipated films in a long time. And they're all together in one book as well (this one, of course!). So what are you waiting for? The Angels' stories begin on the very next page.

© 2000 Academy of Motion Picture Arts and Sciences

Lucy, Cameron, and Drew present at the 72nd Annual Academy Awards

DREW
BARRYMORE

CHAPTER 1

The World's Strongest Angel

Barrymore. Just the name brings instant recognition in the entertainment world. The family Drew Barrymore was born into is a theater and movie dynasty. John Barrymore, Drew's grandfather, has often been called "the greatest lover of the screen." Her grandmother, Dolores Costello Barrymore, was a famed silent-screen actress. Drew's great-aunt, Ethel Barrymore, was a legend on the stage in both England and the United States, and is considered one of the earliest "glamour girls" in the theater world. Even Drew's remarkably good-looking father, John Barrymore, Jr., once seemed to have a promising acting career until drug and alcohol abuse took over his life.

As her work in the movies proves, Drew Barrymore has inherited her family's talent, not to mention their disarming good looks and charm. Those are wonderful gifts for any child to receive. Unfortunately, Drew inherited something quite dangerous from her relatives as well—a tendency toward alcoholism and wild living that some call "the Barrymore curse."

For Drew, the curse struck early. Before she'd even turned fourteen, Drew found herself in a rehabilitation clinic. By fifteen she was legally emancipated from her mother and living on her own.

Why did Drew succumb to the Barrymore curse? Some say it was because she became a world-famous child star, a status that gave Drew access to nightclubs other children didn't have. Many people blame her mother, Jaid Barrymore, for not keeping tighter reins on Drew while she was growing up. In fact it was Jaid who originally brought the young Drew to nightclubs and Hollywood parties. But the truth is, it would be hard to pin the blame on any one person or reason. Drew's troubles came from a combination of issues that she had to eventually overcome.

Drew isn't proud of her wild-child past and she doesn't blame anyone but herself for her past addictions. But she doesn't regret going into acting at a very young age (eleven months, to be exact), either. Now that she has been clean and sober for a long time, Drew says that she is able to view her past problems in a more positive light. Struggling against adversity at a young age has made her a stronger person today.

"I've always seen life as a tree," she once told Oprah Winfrey. "You have your roots and you have the base—the trunk . . . and there are the branches. We can go many different ways to the top of the tree, to our fate."

The branches Drew chose to follow on her tree have turned her into one of the most powerful young women in Hollywood. Not only is she a respected actress, with a talent for both drama and comedy, but she is also a producer of films.

Drew and her partner, Nancy Juvonen, head up Flower Films, a movie production company in California. The company produced its first film, *Never Been Kissed*, in 1998. Being a producer gives Drew a sense of control that she lacked when she was a child. "I didn't want to sit back and wait for things to come to me," she has said. "I wanted to create work for myself."

But don't fool yourself. Drew Barrymore is far from becoming a single-minded businesswoman who is always concerned with the bottom line. Drew is still very much a girl who loves to laugh, and she believes first and foremost that it is "kindness that keeps us going. It's like if we're nice to each other, it really does make the world go around."

By all accounts, Drew is just that—really, really nice. Even as a producer she's the boss we'd all love to have. Especially since she doesn't consider herself anyone's boss. "I put as much patience and understanding [into her job as producer] as I possibly can," she explains. "You have to stick very true to your instincts and choose your battles. Democracy rules. Continue to remain open."

Remain open? That doesn't exactly sound like the way Hollywood usually works. But that's the way Drew works. And she doesn't care if people find it unusual that such a huge star is also a good person who just wants everyone around her to be happy. Despite her Hollywood royalty background, Drew sees herself as just a regular person— well, sort of. Drew does concede that she might be a little sillier than most women her age. But who can blame her? "I get to be a kid now because I wasn't a kid when I was supposed to be one," she asserts. "But in so many ways I am like an old woman—lived it, seen it, done it, been there, have the T-shirt."

Above all, these days Drew loves a good laugh. In fact, her fiancé, Tom Green, is a comedian, which absolutely thrills her. "If I don't have one really good giggle in a day, it wasn't a good day," she insists. "Seriously. I get depressed about that. That'll keep me up at night. I did not laugh enough growing up."

It takes a special kind of person to overcome major obstacles and still emerge as the kind of take-charge woman deserving of the respect Drew Barrymore commands today. Not everyone can defeat their demons. This is the story of one woman who took back her life, and made her past work for her.

© 1999 Laura Luongo/Corbis Outline

Drew takes charge

CHAPTER 2

The Littlest Barrymore

Drew Blythe Barrymore was born on February 22, 1975, in Los Angeles, California. Her parents, Jaid and John, had split up before she even entered the world. John Barrymore was a difficult man with a history of addiction and abuse. After years of putting up with her husband's volatile and sometimes violent behavior, Jaid finally kicked him out of the house when she was pregnant with Drew.

Before Drew was born, Jaid had been a model and an actress herself. But after her beautiful baby girl arrived, Jaid put all her energy into raising her daughter. For a long time they lived in a small ground-floor apartment in West Hollywood. Jaid kept things going by waitressing. And when her friends suggested that she get her dimpled, blond-haired baby into commercials, Jaid resisted. After living with a Barrymore, and having been part of the demanding acting world herself, Jaid was less than thrilled with the idea of having Drew join the family business.

But a friend submitted a picture of Drew to a theatrical agent without Jaid knowing about it. The agent was smitten with the chubby, smiling face in the photo, and by the time she was eleven months old, Drew became the fifth generation of Barrymores to enter the field of professional acting. Her first job was not exactly the stuff legends are made of—it was a Gaines Burgers dog food commercial.

After that, commercials started flowing in fast and furiously. In fact, Drew was chosen for the first four commercials she auditioned for. Once her tiny foot was in the door, it didn't take long for movie producers to become smitten with Drew's big blue eyes and bright smile. At two and a half she got a small role in a TV movie, *Suddenly, Love.* Her character's name was Bobby Graham. Yep, you guessed it. Drew actually played a *boy* in the film. (And you thought Hilary Swank was the first one to pull that off.)

Her role in *Suddenly, Love* wasn't a big one, but Drew was remarkably professional for a two-and-a-half-year-old. As Jaid recalled in Drew's 1990 autobiography,

Little Girl Lost, "Even when she was asleep, her eyes never fluttered. Somehow, at that young age, she understood what it was all about."

Suddenly, Love led to more work for Drew, including small roles in the movies *Altered States* and *Bogie.* Eventually, Jaid quit her job and took on the role of Drew's manager.

When Drew was six years old, Jaid took her to an audition for a part in *Poltergeist,* a movie that was being produced by Steven Spielberg. Unfortunately, as endearing as Drew was during her audition, she just wasn't right for the part of a little girl whose family lives in a haunted house.

Still, Steven Spielberg was charmed by Drew. He kept her in mind when he was casting his next film, a fantasy about an extraterrestrial who becomes stranded on Earth. The movie was called *E.T. The Extra-Terrestrial.*

Steven cast Drew as Gertie, the youngest child in the family that rescues E.T. and helps him find his way home. Drew loved working on *E.T.* There were other children on the set, and Steven Spielberg made acting fun. He let Drew improvise some of her lines, and always took her opinions seriously. For Drew, it was the first time she'd had a male adult in her life. He was like the dad she'd never had. Drew worked hard on the film because every time Steven Spielberg complimented her, she felt proud and happy that she could please this increasingly important father figure.

Drew also loved the E.T. creature. She knew the little alien wasn't real but, like many six-year-old kids, Drew had a vivid imagination. She spent hours talking to the robotic puppet, telling him about her home, and her mom, and the things she liked to do. She even made sure to eat her lunch in the room where E.T. was kept.

To this day, Drew says that working on *E.T. The Extra-Terrestrial* was one of the happiest times in her life. Drew was young then, and acting was like playing pretend. Steven Spielberg never seemed to forget that even though Drew was the consummate professional, she was also a little kid. He made sure that she had fun making the movie.

But the fun and games were about to end. *E.T. The Extra-Terrestrial* went on to become the biggest film of 1982. In fact, it grossed more than $300 million, making it the fourth-highest-grossing film of all time. Drew was singled out for her enchanting portrayal of Gertie, winning a Young Artist

Award and a British Academy of Film and Television Arts Award for her role in the film.

E.T.'s worldwide success brought Drew to a new level of fame. The eight-year-old graduated from child actor to full-fledged celebrity. Producers were fighting to get her to star in their next film. TV was calling, too. In 1983, Drew became the youngest person to ever host *Saturday Night Live*, which meant she was up way past the bedtime of your average eight-year-old.

It was almost ironic. Thanks to a little creature from outer space, Drew's own career had now shot up way into the stratosphere.

© 1982 Universal Pictures/The Neal Peters Collection

The kiss that made a career

Growing Old Before Her Time

Drew's next film was *Irreconcilable Differences*, the story of a little girl who grows so tired of her parents' juvenile behavior that she goes to court to divorce them. (Drew didn't know it at the time, but her own life would soon take a similar path.)

Irreconcilable Differences was a comedy, but Drew didn't have a whole lot of fun making the movie. The director and the producer couldn't seem to agree on anything. That meant there was a lot of tension and yelling going on. This was definitely not the kind of experience Drew had had with the paternal Steven Spielberg at the helm. She was very upset by all the tumultuous anger on the set.

Luckily, once again there was a father figure nearby to give Drew the attention and support she needed. Actor Ryan O'Neal, who played Drew's father in the film, took it upon himself to make sure that the nine-year-old actress had a shoulder to cry on whenever she needed it. Ryan knew how hard life could be for a child star since his own daughter, Tatum, was a child actress herself.

Drew has always had a sense of professionalism that goes way beyond her years ("I love it when people call me an old soul," she admits) and, despite the tensions on the *Irreconcilable Differences* set, she was able to give a phenomenal performance. It was the first time Drew had to carry a whole film on her shoulders, and she rose to the occasion. She did so well, in fact, that she was nominated for a Golden Globe Award for her role as Casey.

© 1984 Warner Bros Inc./The Neal Peters Collection

Although Drew made acting look easy, her life was anything but. Even in school, Drew was finding her newfound stardom difficult. The other kids saw her as

Drew stars in *Irreconcilable Differences*

different now that she was a celebrity. They didn't want to play with her. Some even made fun of her.

"I had just a miserable school experience," she recalled to E! Online. "It was awful. People wouldn't talk to me. I think they just assumed I must be a jerk if I'm an actor. I don't harbor any resentment about that, but it was a lonely experience." At times it was so bad that Drew believed her only real friend was her cat, Gertie, who'd been a gift from Steven Spielberg.

Drew's peers may have steered clear of her, but adult actors and directors loved when she entered their world. She and her mother attended parties at hot spots like L.A.'s Ma Maison and New York City's China Club. She was also a guest at the 1983 Academy Awards. In some ways it was like Drew was living a double life. She was a Hollywood superstar, but she was also a second grader who more than anything just wanted to play the princess in her class's production of *Sleeping Beauty*. (A part she got, making her even less popular with the kids in her school.)

That dual existence began to get the best of Drew by the time she turned ten. She continued working at a frenzied schedule, starring alongside big-name stars like George C. Scott in the Stephen King thriller *Firestarter*, and James Woods in *Cat's Eye*. On the set, she was a total professional, getting there on time and knowing her lines. But off-camera, Drew was already beginning to spin out of control.

To make matters worse, as Drew hit adolescence she got fewer and fewer calls from directors. She was at an awkward stage physically, and the scripts she was receiving were less than stellar. That meant more than a loss of income to Drew. Movie sets were like home to her. On the sets, people paid attention to Drew. Directors like Steven Spielberg and Dino De Laurentiis were like surrogate fathers to her. "Work was my saving grace," she wrote in *Little Girl Lost*. "The one tangible thing I could always rely on to boost my sagging self-esteem and confidence."

Drew's professional support system was slowly disappearing as the time between roles became longer and longer. Her dependencies grew stronger. And she found a new addiction—food.

"I had a really bad weight problem," she remembers of her preteen years. "I looked like a butterball; couldn't even get a job because I was so fat. . . . Finally, when I was twelve, my agents sat me down and said, 'you have to lose this weight.'"

Deep down, Drew knew that she wasn't eating because she was hungry. She was eating to replace something that was missing in her life. "Some people say that being fat might be psychological. And I believe in my heart that it was with me," she admits.

Drew soon began hanging around with an older crowd of kids in their late teens. The seventeen- and eighteen-year-olds liked doing the same things Drew liked—going clubbing, and staying out really late. It wasn't hard for Drew's new friends to look old enough to fake their way into clubs and bars. And even though Drew was not yet thirteen, club owners always waved her through—it was good publicity to have the star of *E.T.* in their clubs.

It seemed as though the adults around Drew were not aware of her habits. She continued to make whatever movies she could, and to do her schoolwork (although she admits she didn't try too hard to get good grades). And even though she was often photographed dancing in clubs at two in the morning, no one in her life tried to give her a curfew.

Eventually, Drew's habitual abuse left her unable to cope with other people. The once work-hungry actress had very little ambition left. As she explained in *Little Girl Lost*, "That's the insidious nature of [addiction]. You always want more, more, more."

As Drew herself recalled in her autobiography, there came a point where she tried to tell herself, "Get a grip girl." But it was too late.

Drew's life finally spun completely out of control on June 28, 1988. She had a huge fight with her mother over what Drew perceived as Jaid's lack of respect for her independence. By the end of the battle, Drew actually ordered Jaid out of the house they shared.

Jaid finally faced up to the fact that Drew had a problem, and took her daughter to the ASAP Family Treatment Center in Los Angeles. There was no alternative. If she kept going the way she was, there was a good chance that Drew Barrymore would be dead before she ever reached her fourteenth birthday.

CHAPTER 4

Taking Control

Going through the rehab program at ASAP was perhaps the hardest thing Drew has ever had to do. Not only did she have to deal with the physical problems of cleaning her body, she had to face her emotional problems head-on. While she was allowed to work for short periods of time during her stay at ASAP (shooting the film *Far from Home* and looping dialogue for *See You in the Morning*, a movie she'd almost completed before entering rehab), she spent her days for the most part working with counselors (many of whom were recovering addicts themselves) to come to terms with issues. It wasn't easy, but Drew had to cope with the fact that her father wasn't the responsible family man she fantasized about, and she had to learn to try to forgive her mother for being more like an agent than a parent. Mostly, though, she had to learn to take responsibility for her own actions.

While Drew had been able to use her acting talent to fool people in the outside world about her addiction, she couldn't pull any fast ones on the counselors at ASAP. And so, Drew was forced to face her demons at what often seemed like an endless string of therapy sessions and exercises. She was also forced to follow a schedule—which included an early 7:30 wake-up call. For the sleep-loving Drew, getting to lie in bed in the morning was a luxury she missed a lot.

Although initially many kids at the center feared that Drew would get special treatment because she was a movie star, Drew did make several friends at the center. Stripped of her professional status, Drew was just another recovering addict. For the first time, she was pretty much one of the gang.

But outside the center, Drew was still a hot commodity. And her story was the kind that tabloid journalists salivate over. On January 3, 1989, just a few days after she was released from ASAP, *The National Enquirer* ran a story about her stay at the clinic.

Drew was furious and decided to fight back. She told her story to *People* magazine. She wanted the truth out there, not the lies the tabloids would make up.

Drew's story brought mixed reviews from the magazine's readership. Many adults had trouble mustering any sympathy for Drew. But teens seemed to understand where she was coming from—several even suggested that Drew had inspired them to go for help themselves.

Drew went back to work on an ABC After-School Special called *Getting Straight*, about teenage drug use. Ironically, much of the movie, which costarred Corey Haim and Tatum O'Neal, was filmed at the ASAP Center Drew had just left.

As most recovering addicts will tell you, you're never really cured of a drug or alcohol addiction. It's a constant uphill battle—and in Drew's case, it's a battle she almost lost. A few months after leaving ASAP, Drew fell back into her old habits. By July she was back living at the ASAP Center.

While at ASAP, Drew began writing an autobiography. That would be unusual for most teenagers, but Drew was far from an average kid. In her fourteen years she'd experienced more than most adults ever would. Drew worked with Todd Gold, the reporter who had helped her with the *People* article about her first stint in rehab. When *Little Girl Lost* was released in 1990, it was an instant hit, eventually reaching number one on *The New York Times* Best-seller List.

Drew emerged from ASAP ready to go back to work. Unfortunately, Hollywood wasn't quite as ready to work with her. Producers, directors, and insurance companies were afraid that Drew was too much of a risk to hire.

Drew took whatever work she could find, playing roles in forgettable films like *Waxwork II: Lost in Time* and *Motorama*. Drew's career was going nowhere. At one point she even took on a job as a waitress in a coffee shop—a profession she had absolutely no talent for at all.

It was around this time that Drew decided she could no longer live with Jaid. Their relationship was strained, and Drew knew that being in the same house with her mother was detrimental to her well-being. At age fifteen Drew left home and got an apartment with a friend. She even went so far as to have herself declared an emancipated minor—essentially divorcing herself from her mother.

"My mom and I, we're like oil and water," Drew explained some years later. "We just don't mix."

Despite Drew's reputation, in 1991

writer-director Katt Shea decided to take a chance on her. She cast her in the title role of her new film, *Poison Ivy*.

Drew had a tough time playing the role of Ivy in the adult drama. She was definitely playing against type. And not just her Hollywood type (although she was certain that a lot of people would be shocked that the girl who had once played sweet little Gertie was now portraying a completely amoral, sensuous creature, capable of destroying an entire family). Drew was also playing against the type of person she is inside.

"It was really hard for me," she recalls of playing Ivy. "I'm wicked in that movie. It was hard being Ivy for three months. I thought I would go crazy inside. I'm a nice person. She's like the evilest woman in the world and sometimes I felt like I was going crazy."

But there was a part of Drew that enjoyed the challenge of playing someone so incredibly mean. "I like to do pieces that are different," she admits. "I don't want to play myself because, boy, I get to be me my whole life."

Poison Ivy was the break Drew needed. Reviews of the film itself were mixed, but critics loved Drew's performance in the film. The *Washington Post* said that Drew had "grown into a very sexy, very interesting young actress."

Following her success in *Poison Ivy*, Drew took on the role of Anita in *Guncrazy*. In the movie, Anita, a small-town girl, develops a pen pal relationship with a convict. When Anita's "friend" is sprung from prison, he takes her on a wild killing spree.

Drew's portrayal of Anita earned her a Golden Globe Award nomination, and the respect of the Hollywood elite. Even *The New York Times*' tough-to-please film critic Vincent Canby raved that "Drew Barrymore gives the kind of performance that can transform a sweetly competent actress into a major screen personality."

Drew's newfound adult career included a stint on television as well, portraying Lindsay in the 1992 series *2000 Malibu Road*. Unfortunately, the series did not score the ratings needed to make it a success, and it was canceled before the 1992–93 TV season came to a close.

Drew's next high-profile role was a 1993 made-for-TV movie called *Beyond Control: The Amy Fisher Story*. In 1992 and 1993, it was impossible to turn on the TV without hearing the name Amy Fisher. She was the "Long Island Lolita" who'd had a relationship with an older man named Joey Buttafuoco and tried to kill his wife in the hopes that Joey would marry her. The Amy Fisher story captivated the country, so much so that the three major television networks all planned movies based on the saga.

Three well-respected actresses were cast as Amy in the dueling movies—Alyssa Milano (*Casualty of Love*), Noelle Parker (*Treachery in the Suburbs: The Amy Fisher Story*), and Drew (*Beyond Control: The Amy Fisher Story*). Of the three films, *Beyond Control* was arguably the most objective, since it was based on the experiences of *New York Post* reporter Amy Pagnozzi, who had covered the case for her newspaper. The other two films were based on the memories of the people involved: Amy Fisher (*Treachery in the Suburbs*) and Mary Jo and Joey Buttafuoco (*Casualty of Love*). Drew's performance in *her* film garnered her great praise, particularly for the braveness of her decision to portray Amy as a sympathetic character. As *Cosmopolitan* magazine put it, "she performs the impossible by making Amy likable."

Drew seemed to understand the emotions

that drove Amy Fisher, even if she didn't condone her actions. That's what made Drew the perfect actress to play a troubled teen. "Drew put on a wig and she just became Amy Fisher," executive producer Andrew Adelson recalled to *Entertainment Weekly* in late 1992. "She was perfect for the part."

The success of *Beyond Control: The Amy Fisher Story* secured Drew's reclaimed status as an actress in demand in Hollywood. And as her career got back on course, Drew's sense of self-worth also grew stronger. She was no longer the angry, scared, thirteen-year-old who had entered the ASAP Family Treatment Center. She'd made her peace with the past.

"I'm not the only child in the world that feels let down by their parents," she told *GQ* magazine. "That's the way it is. I'm related to these people, there's certainly no question about that. Now maybe I've broken the cycle that they had. I feel further and further away from that every day."

Finally, the *Little Girl Lost* appeared to have found her way.

CHAPTER 5

Today's Drew

As the twentieth century came to an end, Drew was in a wonderful stage of her life. The year 2000 found her emotionally stronger than ever. She had come to terms with the fact she would never have much of a relationship bond with either of her parents. She hardly ever heard from her father— and when she did, it was usually because he needed money. And if there was ever any chance of mother and daughter becoming close again, Jaid may have been the one to blow it. In 1999 Jaid went through her attic and discovered items from Drew's childhood. Eventually she ran an online auction to sell off Drew's infant clothing and movie memorabilia to fans, including the red cowboy hat Drew wore in *E.T. The Extra-Terrestrial*.

It's hard to say what Drew's feelings about Jaid's auction really were. She never publicly commented on her mother's actions. But if she was disappointed, she was probably not surprised. After all, Jaid had made a whole career out of being a celebrity's mother.

Drew learned to compensate for her lack of family life by surrounding herself with a group of friends that satisfied her inner wild child without enticing her to do things that were harmful to her body.

"They're in control of their lives," Drew says of her friends today. "I mean obviously it wouldn't be in my best interest to hang around with (the wrong crowd). But I don't need to be with somebody who's General Patton about it either."

One of the members of Drew's inner circle is Nancy Juvonen. In 1995, she and Drew joined forces to create Flower Films, a production company. The two young women started out with nothing more than a laptop and a book of phone numbers. Today, Flower Films is a major Hollywood player, with offices on Sunset Boulevard in West Hollywood. The first film produced by the company, *Never Been Kissed*, was released in 1999.

The new Drew was a businesswoman who was also starring in hit films like *Boys on the Side* and *Batman Forever*. The tabloids no longer had her drug and alcohol habits to write about. And news of Drew's ever-growing collection of tattoos—she has six at

In control: Drew and Nancy Juvonen styling at the *Never Been Kissed* premiere

the moment—didn't seem to be big news. But the tabloids loved running stories about Drew, so in the 1990s the papers turned to covering her romantic life instead.

Drew gave the tabloid reporters plenty to write about. She dated a number of young Hollywood hotties, and even became engaged to actor James Walters in 1992. But the couple split up before they ever reached the aisle.

None of Drew's dating escapades ever made headlines the way her March 1994 marriage to Hollywood club owner Jeremy Thomas did. The couple had dated only five weeks before Drew proposed to Jeremy. That very night they looked through the phone book and found a female "psychic priest" who married them a few hours later in The Room, one of Jeremy's bars. At the time, Drew told a reporter for *GQ* that she was excited because, "I have another half, you know? Which I love. I love this person."

But the love didn't last. Six weeks later, the couple split up. Within a year, their divorce was final.

After her divorce, Drew still loved the dating scene. For a while she was attached to Hole guitarist Eric Erlandson, and later actor Luke Wilson. Today, the man in Drew's life is MTV comedy show host Tom Green. Drew first met Tom in November 1999, when she asked him to do a cameo role as a boat captain in *Charlie's Angels*. Their attraction was automatic. But it wasn't until Drew supported Tom through his battle with testicular cancer in early 2000 that the two became inseparable.

By the summer of 2000, Tom decided to take their relationship to the next level. On July 8, while walking the beach in magnificent Malibu, California, Tom proposed to Drew, and presented her with a gorgeous Tiffany engagement ring. She accepted immediately.

© 2000 Fitzroy Barrett/Globe Photos Inc.

A kiss from future hubby, Tom Green

The joy in Drew's personal life is equaled only by the success of her current film career—she's a big Hollywood player now, both as an actress and as a producer.

As an actress, she fulfilled a childhood dream by getting the chance to work with Woody Allen, when she played Skylar in *Everyone Says I Love You* in 1996. "To me that was a gift," she says of playing a comedic debutante in the movie. "Talk about a fairy tale. . . . I auditioned many times and it was really hard for Woody to see me as a debutante, but I completely understood that I could do this character. And [Woody Allen] is someone I grew up watching."

Later that year she took on the small role of Casey in the movie *Scream*, even though she'd been offered the lead role that later went to Neve Campbell. For Drew, the decision to take on the smaller part was a no-brainer. She simply liked the character better.

Scream was a lot of fun for Drew to make, because she's a huge fan of scary movies. "I love slasher films," she admitted to Oprah Winfrey. "They're my favorite. [Making *Scream*] was so cathartic. You're screaming and crying for ten days straight . . . I released the demons. I cleared every bad thing that ever happened to me. I've never felt so free."

Scream went on to become one of the biggest hits of 1996, and spawned two sequels. Drew wasn't in either of those, however, since her character had been killed off early in the first film. (FYI: Don't look for Casey to reemerge one day in any future *Scream* flicks. "I think it's best for Casey Becker to stay in the grave," Drew joked during an interview with E! Online. "She's happy there, by the way. She and the earthworms are just hittin' it off like a house afire.")

That's Drew's sense of humor—silly and a little offbeat. She's used that sense of humor in recent years to turn herself into a phenomenal comedic actress. Her 1998 performance as Julia Sullivan in *The Wedding Singer* proved

© 1999 Jeff Slocomb/Corbis Outline

Sometimes a spaz . . .

that. After making the Adam Sandler film, Drew was nominated for a Funniest Actress in a Motion Picture award from the American Comedy Awards. (She and Adam also won an MTV Movie Award for Best Kiss.)

After *The Wedding Singer*, Drew took on the starring role of Danielle in *Ever After*, the 1998 remake of *Cinderella*, for which she won a Saturn Award for Best Actress from the Academy of Science Fiction, Horror and Fantasy Films. After finishing the feminist version of the popular fairy tale, Drew went to work as executive producer and star of a contemporary comedy called *Never Been Kissed*.

Unlike the romantic, glamorous, empowered heroine of *Ever After*, Drew's character in *Never Been Kissed* was a total dweeb. In fact, in various scenes in the film, Drew wore incredibly bad hair and had a face filled with (phony) zits. Her character, Josie Geller (or "Josie Grossy"), was also a major klutz. But Drew didn't mind the bad makeup or pratfalls. In fact, she seemed to revel in it.

"Listen, if I can make someone laugh, I think that's the best thing in the world," she told *Entertainment Tonight*. "For some reason, when you laugh, everything else just dissipates and for a few minutes in your day, the burdens and the worries just go away . . . it's really nice when you get to lose them for a second."

By all accounts, the set of *Never Been Kissed* was filled with laughs. The good humor and positive atmosphere all seemed to filter down from the top. Drew was happy, and therefore the cast and crew were as well.

Keeping the people who work on her movies happy is one of Drew's biggest priorities. "[Hollywood] is a shallow . . . cruel world," she explains. "I like making movies, so I want to make good movies. I want to swim in a creative pool with wonderful people. And as a producer, I want to create a great working atmosphere for people. I know how to do that. It's in my blood and in my bones."

Making "good movies" is something Drew has shown that she is completely capable of doing. The Flower Films project that followed *Never Been Kissed* was a 1999 animated TV special called *Olive, the Other Reindeer*, which was based on a popular children's book. Drew voiced the lead character of Olive, a dog who wants to be a reindeer and help Santa.

Drew shows no signs of slowing down in 2000. Flower Films has grown to be a major force in Hollywood. She and Nancy Juvonen are producing two films in 2000, and Drew stars in both of them. In *So Love Returns*, Drew plays a woman who magically appears from the ocean to help a young writer whose world crumbles when his wife passes away. And Flower Films is also the producing force behind *Charlie's Angels*.

It seems only right that Drew should be making *Charlie's Angels* right now. After all, the film is about powerful women, and that's just what Drew has become. Despite all the adversity life has thrown at her, Drew Barrymore has risen up and taken

© 1998 Steve Granitz/Retna Limited, USA

A real Angel

control of her own destiny. And she's done it without ever becoming bitter about the past. In fact, she embraces the hard times, because they allow her to really appreciate where she is right now.

"I never regret anything," she insists. "Because every little detail of your life is what made you into who you are in the end."

Clue In to Drew

Drew Barrymore's life has been a series of ups and downs—but all of those experiences have gone into making her the vibrant, take-charge woman she is today. How much do you know about the details that make up Drew's life? Find out by trying your hand at this Drew Barrymore quiz. Some answers can be found in this book; others can't. But don't worry if you can't answer them all; you can check your answers on page 48. When you're all through, you'll find out just how much you knew about Drew.

1. Who were Pizza and Little Gertie?

2. Drew is godmother to what actress-singer's daughter?

3. What is Drew's favorite flower?

4. Kids in grade school taunted Drew with which of these nicknames?
A. E.T. B. Drew the Poo C. The Diva

5. Which Steven Spielberg film did Drew audition for before *E.T.?*

6. True or false: When choosing a dress for the 2000 Academy Awards, Drew insisted that her dressmaker cover the angel tattoo on her back.

7. What is the name of Drew's production company?

8. Drew's first professional gig was a commercial for what?
A. Gaines Burgers dog food B. Mr. Bubble bubble bath C. Ivory soap

9. What job did Drew's character have in *Never Been Kissed?*

10. Who was John Barrymore?

11. What is Drew's middle name?

12. Which "Long Island Lolita" did Drew play in a 1993 made-for-TV movie?

13. In which Batman movie did Drew play Sugar?
A. *Batman and Robin* B. *Batman* C. *Batman Forever*

14. True or false: Drew is a natural brunette.

15. Who is Drew's favorite poet?
A. Dylan Thomas B. Emily Dickinson C. e. e. cummings

16. True or false: Drew is a strict vegan who won't eat meat, fish, eggs, or dairy.

17. Who does Drew's character Casey try to divorce in *Irreconcilable Differences*?

18. Which of her childhood costars did Drew describe as "huggable"?

19. What late-night talk show host has Drew had a crush on since she was a kid? A. Conan O'Brien B. Jay Leno C. David Letterman

20. Which of Drew's movie memorabilia did her mother recently attempt to auction off on the Internet for $45,000?

Answers to the Clue In to Drew Quiz

1. Drew's childhood cats
2. Courtney Love's little girl, Frances Bean Cobain
3. The daisy
4. B
5. *Poltergeist*
6. False. She wanted it to show.
7. Flower Films
8. A
9. She was a newspaper copyeditor.
10. A famous actor who was Drew's grandfather. (Her dad is John Barrymore, Jr.)

11. Blythe
12. Amy Fisher in *Beyond Control: The Amy Fisher Story*
13. C
14. True
15. C
16. True
17. Her parents
18. *Firestarter*'s George C. Scott
19. C
20. Her red cowboy hat from *E.T.*

How'd You Do?

15–20 correct: Whoa! What an awesome score. Drew is obviously the Angel for you.

9–14 correct: Consider yourself a Drew expert.

5–8 correct: Your score could use a little help. But this is not an irreconcilable difference. You can always reread this book and take the test again!

0–4 correct: You seem to have missed the whole Drew Barrymore phenomenon. Are you an E.T. or something?

CHAPTER 7

Drew's Filmography

Suddenly, Love (1978) (TV) . . . Bobby Graham

Altered States (1980) . . . Margaret Jessup

Bogie (1980) (TV) . . . Leslie Bogart

E.T. the Extra-Terrestrial (1982) . . . Gertie

Irreconcilable Differences (1984) . . . Casey
  Brodsky

Firestarter (1984) . . . Charlie McGee

Cat's Eye (1985) . . . Amanda

Babes in Toyland (1986) (TV) . . . Lisa Piper

Conspiracy of Love (1987) (TV) . . . Jody
  Woldarski

See You in the Morning (1989) . . . Cathy

Far from Home (1989) . . . Joleen Cox

Waxwork II: Lost in Time (1992) . . .Vampire
  Victim

Poison Ivy (1992) . . . Ivy

No Place to Hide (1992) . . . Tinsel Hanley

Motorama (1992) . . . Fantasy Girl

Sketch Artist (1992) (TV) . . . Daisy

2000 Malibu Road (1992) (TV series) . . .
  Lindsay

Guncrazy (1992) . . . Anita Minteer

Doppelganger: The Evil Within (1992) . . . Holly
   Gooding

Beyond Control: The Amy Fisher Story (1993) (TV)
   . . . Amy Fisher

Wayne's World 2 (1993) . . . Bjergen Kjergen

Inside the Goldmine (1994) . . . Daisy

Boys on the Side (1995) . . . Holly

Mad Love (1995) . . . Casey Roberts

Batman Forever (1995) . . . Sugar

Everyone Says I Love You (1996) . . . Skylar

Scream (1996) . . . Casey Becker

Wishful Thinking (1997) . . . Lena

Best Men (1997) . . . Hope

The Wedding Singer (1998) . . . Julia Sullivan

Ever After (1998) . . . Danielle De Barbarac

Home Fries (1998) . . . Sally

Never Been Kissed (1999) . . . Josie Gellar

Olive the Other Reindeer (1999) (TV—voice only)
   . . . Olive

Titan A.E. (2000) (voice only) . . . Akima

Charlie's Angels: The Movie (2000) . . . Dylan

So Love Returns (2000)

CAMERON
DIAZ

CHAPTER 8

Just an Actress . . . Finally

When Cameron Diaz walked out onto the
stage to present the first Oscar of 2000, it
marked a major milestone in her career. That
night, Cameron knew for certain that she
was considered an actress worthy of being
on the same stage with Hollywood legends
like Jane Fonda, Warren Beatty, and Billy
Crystal. She was one of them.

Ever since Cameron began acting, she'd
seen the same adjectives next to her name
whenever it appeared in print: Model-
Turned-Actress Cameron Diaz. It had gotten
to the point that Cameron could barely
stand to see the words. It's not that the title
wasn't accurate. After all, Cameron had
indeed been an Elite model who'd appeared
on runways and magazine covers all over
the world before trying her hand at acting. It
was just that it'd been a long time since
Cameron had done any modeling. Her film
career, on the other hand, was huge. She'd

been in many hit films, like *The Mask*, *She's the One*, and *My Best Friend's Wedding*. And of course there was the smash hit *There's Something About Mary*, which earned Cameron a Best Actress Award from the prestigious New York Film Critics Circle.

So if her career was moving along so well, why did Cameron so desperately want the phrase Model-Turned-Actress to be permanently severed from her name?

"People just assume you don't have the ability to think," she explains about being tagged a model.

© 1999 Armando Gallo/Reina Limited, USA

More than a pretty face

It's hard to break out of the mold that the Hollywood press builds for you. And so for a long time, despite all of Cameron's successes, the Model-Turned-Actress title stuck. But little by little, reviewers began spending more time talking about her acting and less time going on about her looks. Then, in 1999,

Cameron took on a role that would make it quite clear that she was more than just a pretty face.

In *Being John Malkovich*, the cult hit about a group of people who find a way to enter actor John Malkovich's brain, Cameron played Lotte Schwartz—a character whose frizzy hair and bad complexion wiped away any thoughts of Cameron-the-model. *Being John Malkovich* became one of the most raved about films of 1999. Everyone who was anyone was talking about the movie—and how daring Cameron was for purposely making herself unattractive on camera. Cameron knew that from that moment on, Model-Turned-Actress would be a thing of the past.

And so, with a résumé of big hits and well-reviewed independent films behind her, Cameron stepped out on the stage of the Shrine Auditorium alongside her fellow Charlie's Angels, Drew Barrymore and Lucy Liu, and presented the Best Costume Design Award. There she was, standing before the Hollywood elite as one of them. She was an actress, plain and simple. Well, not quite plain and simple. Because as you will soon learn, nothing has ever been simple in Cameron Diaz's life.

CHAPTER 9

A Real Tomboy

Cameron Diaz was born on August 30, 1972, in the community of Long Beach, California. Long Beach is one of those California towns you see in movies—dotted with palm trees, and located near the ocean.

Growing up, Cameron lived in a two-story middle-class gray stucco house with her dad, Emilio, an oil foreman; her mom, Billie, an import-export agent; and her older sister, Chimene. Cameron's father was the one who chose his younger daughter's unusual name. He just liked the sound of the word *Cameron*, which is a Gaelic expression meaning "crooked stream."

Even by tough California standards, Cameron was a striking beauty. She was the perfect combination of her Cuban-American father and her German, English, and Native American mother. But Cameron wasn't one of those girls who grew up in front of the mirror, keenly aware of her looks. In fact,

Cameron was more into playing ball outside than trying on her mother's nail polish. Growing up, Cameron's fashion statement was scraped knees—battle scars from playing ball on hard asphalt surfaces—which she wore with pride.

Cameron credits her laissez-faire attitude toward beauty to her mom, who never put an emphasis on faces and figures. "I was fortunate that I grew up with my mom, who I never heard once complain about her body," Cameron explains.

Looking at Cameron now, with her designer gowns and perfect makeup, it's hard to picture her as the tough-kid tomboy she swears she really was while growing up in Long Beach.

"I'm always thought of as girlie," she admits. "But that's never been the truth. I grew up as a tomboy. I've always liked action."

Action, in Cameron's case, included playing ball, and mastering the skateboard—which she proudly rode all the way to the local mall.

All those stops at the mall's food court never seemed to affect the athletic Cameron. She rose to her current five feet nine inches seemingly without gaining any weight at all.

Her thin, thin, *thin* frame led the other kids to call her "Skeletor." While the name may have hurt, tough-girl Cameron never let on. Instead of giving in to the kids who taunted her, Cameron simply, "kicked the_____out of them!"

Now keep in mind that it wasn't that Cameron was *trying* to stay super thin as a kid. She simply didn't gain weight. Cameron has always been blessed with an incredibly fast metabolism. She can eat anything, and frequently does. "I just love french fries," she admits. "Some people are chocolate and sweets people. I love french fries . . . and caviar."

Okay, so maybe her tastes have changed a little since she's grown up.

Even though Cameron recalls thinking of herself as a "total heavy metal chick" who spent her childhood in jeans and flannel shirts—her mother took her to her first Van Halen concert—the truth is that her desire to be an actress was always part of her makeup. As early as second grade, Cameron recalls dressing up as Mae West for a school Halloween pageant. Even her high school heavy metal persona displayed an early flair for taking on a character—Cameron always seemed to be dressed for the part, complete with dark black eyeliner; long, feathered hair; and the ever-present bandanna in her back jeans pocket.

That's not exactly the look most talent agents search for when they're scouting for girls who could become models. But Cameron's unique beauty shone through the dark mascara and hair bleach. At age sixteen, she was discovered by a photographer named Jeff Dumas.

"Cameron had a sparkle," Jeff recalled in *People* magazine.

In Hollywood, lots of guys try to impress girls by saying they're fashion photographers. A beauty like Cameron had definitely heard that one before. Usually, after a guy tried that line on her, Cameron left him high and dry. But there was something about Jeff that made Cameron believe that he was the real deal.

"He asked to speak to my father," she explained to *People.*

Within a week of being discovered by Jeff, Cameron had a meeting with the talent people at the famed Elite modeling agency. Cameron's unique facial structure, piercing blue eyes, and knockout body caught their attention, too. They wanted to give Cameron a contract. Cameron's parents were okay with the idea—as long as their daughter graduated from Long Beach Polytechnic High School, the school she was attending at the time. Cameron agreed to the bargain and stayed in school, graduating in 1989 with above average grades.

Cameron's first modeling job was in a print ad for *Teen* magazine. It wasn't exactly a supermodel gig. In fact, it paid only $125. But, hey, everyone's got to start somewhere.

Cameron was on her way.

CHAPTER 10

On Her Own

Imagine being just out of high school and on your own in an exotic foreign country. Sounds like the perfect fantasy life, right? Well, that's just what happened to Cameron when she was eighteen years old. The Elite modeling agency sent her off to Japan for a photo shoot to start off her modeling career.

When Cameron left for Japan, her mother gave her a very special gift, a long silver hairpin. But her mother wasn't just passing along the pin for style's sake. She had completely different intentions. "It's beautiful—and it can be used as a weapon," Cameron once explained to *People* magazine. "Moms are like that."

Cameron's mom wasn't exactly worrying needlessly. After all, her daughter was about to be on her own for the very first time. Learning to be responsible for your own actions can take a little time. Most people learn their lessons the hard way. Cameron was no exception.

"You can get into a lot of trouble being in a foreign country with no adult telling you when to come home," she admits.

After learning from experience, Cameron got smart and limited her partying severely. Besides, once the modeling offers started coming in, Cameron discovered that she had less and less time for fun. After all, despite the way it appears, modeling is a tough job. You have to look perfect just about all the time, even when you're not being photographed. You have to put your best foot forward when you go out on rounds (meetings in which you have to introduce yourself to clients) to convince them you're the right girl for their product. That's pretty hard to do when you're not well rested. Cameron had the added difficulty of not being classified into a specific "type." Her looks were very unique, and not always what the clients had in mind.

"I knew I wasn't the prettiest girl," Cameron recalled to *Harper's Bazaar* of her days spent sitting with the other models in clients' waiting rooms. "But I would go in and have a great time with the clients. I made them laugh. They wanted to know that they'd have a good time and not be stuck with some prima donna model type."

Whether or not she was the prettiest girl around is obviously debatable, since the always modest Cameron can't exactly be called upon to be an objective critic of herself. Still, Cameron must have been doing something right. Before long, she was flying all over the world, filming Coke commercials in Australia, and appearing on the covers of magazines like *Seventeen* and *Mademoiselle*. At one point in her modeling career, Cameron was earning upward of two thousand dollars a day for her work. It just goes to prove that a great personality can take you a long way. (Of course in Cameron's case, those blazing baby blues probably didn't hurt, either.)

It was while she was on one of her modeling gigs that Cameron met a video producer named Carlos De La Torre. In 1990, Cameron was working in Japan on a job that Carlos was coordinating. There was an instant attraction between the two. At one point Cameron admits that she and Carlos talked about marriage. But at eighteen, Cameron was far from ready for marriage. Still, the couple were together for almost five years. They split up in 1995.

Cameron loved modeling. After all, as she

© 1997 Jim Cooper/Retna Limited, USA

A natural in front of the camera

told *Vogue,* "I got to travel all over the world and meet interesting people." But deep in her heart, Cameron knew that she was not heading for supermodel status. "I never got the work I wanted," she told *Premiere* magazine. "I only worked twice when I was in Paris, and I lived there for nine months."

Besides, there was an artistic side of her that was not being fulfilled in the modeling world. Cameron needed an outlet for her creativity. The question was, what art form would Cameron focus her efforts on?

Cameron remembered liking her high school drama class, and decided to give acting a shot. A film career seemed like the perfect segue from modeling—her on-camera modeling experience could only help Cameron in the acting world.

The first script Cameron read was for a Jim Carrey project called *The Mask*. The role Cameron wanted to audition for was a small one; just a few scenes as a steamy lounge singer. But while the part was small, the movie was going to be a big-budget number with lots of special effects. Cameron knew that if she could get the part, it would be her break into the acting world. So she put on a brave face and went to read for the role of Tina Carlyle.

CHAPTER 11

An Independent Thinker

By choosing *The Mask* as her first big audition, Cameron was definitely not taking the easy way out. It seemed every beautiful girl in Hollywood wanted that role—even though it was filmed before the release of *Ace Ventura, Pet Detective*, the film that made Jim Carrey a household name. To make matters worse, Cameron was not the type of girl the film's producers had in mind for the role of Tina Carlyle. The producers weren't looking for a skinny model type for the part. They wanted someone with plenty of curves. Resourceful Cameron overcame that hurdle with the purchase of a thirty-six-dollar padded bra.

But even with her newly enhanced body, Cameron still had to convince the producers that she could act. It took her twelve auditions to prove that one. "Getting the audition for *The Mask* was luck," Cameron recalled to *Movieline*. "Earning it was work."

So much work that Cameron developed an ulcer during the audition process. But she kept on trying for the role, and eventually it was hers.

The Mask earned more than $100 million in the United States alone. Audiences and critics alike seemed to love the film's offbeat, wacky, cartoon humor. The reviews for Cameron were especially terrific. Even the unpredictable critic Roger Ebert (co-originator of the thumbs-up thumbs-down review) called her "a genuine sex bomb with a gorgeous face, a wonderful smile, and a gift of comic timing."

Ironically, Cameron's lack of superstardom success in the modeling world may have helped her out with reviewers. When a supermodel tries her hand at acting, Hollywood critics are usually poised to go on the attack, eager to prove that modeling is a breeze compared to what it takes to be an actress. But in Cameron's case, she wasn't well known at all. Most of the critics had no clue who she was. *Before* the film that is. Once *The Mask* hit theaters, it seemed everyone knew the name Cameron Diaz.

Okay, once you've been in a hit movie, all of your next films will be big-studio deals, with huge budgets and lots of press attention, right? Wrong. What Cameron soon discovered was that if you really wanted to learn the craft of acting, the big studios were not the way to go. The studios all wanted to cash in on a sure thing, asking Cameron to go the bombshell route in film after film. But Cameron wasn't interested in getting typecast. So she turned down the big names and turned to smaller productions. Cameron knew that the real opportunities for juicy roles that stretched her acting chops could be found in independent films. And although the salaries were much smaller than the studio jobs, Cameron decided "indies" were the way to go.

"It's easy once you play a sex symbol to go along and play every role that way. But I decided if I was going to be in this for the long haul and really get something out of acting—what I wanted out of it—I was going to have to make the decision of waiting to get a part that could show people I can do other things. It was a definite conscious decision," she says of going the independent film route.

Besides, Cameron knew that she still had a lot to learn. She wanted acting to be a lifelong career, not something as short-lived as the typical modeling career. To ensure that she would be working well into her thirties, forties, and fifties, she had to become a real actress, not just a pretty face splashed across the silver screen. "I think that definitely your chances of coming across material . . . that is more interesting and more challenging is more likely [in independent films] than it is in big-studio films," she explains. "You always have to leave your doors open to independent films."

With that in mind, Cameron followed up her role in *The Mask* with the part of Jude in a small independent feature called *The Last Supper*. Jude was the complete opposite of Tina. Tina was bold and totally wild, while Jude was icy and uptight. To play the part, Cameron dressed down and ditched the padding in favor of her own body.

Cameron's decision to go with a low-profile, well-written, independent film absolutely had the desired effect on her career. Filmmakers came knocking on her door, begging her to take on more complex roles. She followed up *The Last Supper* with *Feeling Minnesota*. In that flick she costarred with Keanu Reeves, who was still on a Hollywood high thanks to his success in the thriller *Speed*. Cameron played Freddie, a woman who comes between two brothers.

Cameron was not the first name that came to mind when the film's director, Steven Baigelman, was casting the role in his film. In fact, "She seemed completely the opposite of what I wanted," Steven recalled in *People* magazine.

But Cameron showed Steven that she was the type of actress who could be anyone he wanted her to be. To prove it, she dyed her naturally blond hair dark brown, and took on a far darker personality as well. Eventually she found herself on a plane to Minnesota, ready to begin filming.

Like most independent films, *Feeling Minnesota* was not exactly a blockbuster at the box office. But Cameron got something more valuable than money out of the experience.

"Keanu and [fellow costar]

A darker look for Cameron

Vincent [D'Onofrio] taught me a lot about focus and concentration," she told the *L.A.*

Daily News. "They were also very honest with their characters, so I learned that."

Besides, a film's financial success has never been very important to Cameron. "I personally could care less about the box office success of a film," she told *Premiere.* "That's the media. It's always noted what a film does."

The film may not have been a box office biggie, but Cameron's notices were quite good. Roger Ebert exclaimed in his *Chicago Sun-Times* column that "Cameron Diaz is the discovery here. I first became aware of her in *The Mask* in which she was a siren. . . . Now after seeing her in movies like *The Last Supper* and *She's the One,* and in this lead role in *Feeling Minnesota,* I realize she has range and comic ability."

Feeling Minnesota brought Cameron a reputation as a versatile actress who was willing to go the extra mile for a role. It also brought a new friendship with actor Matt Dillon, who was on location in Minnesota at the same time, filming an independent feature called *Beautiful Girls.*

Matt was immediately attracted to Cameron, but she was more cautious since she was still fresh from her breakup with Carlos De La Torre. Still, the two hung out in their hotel together and became fast friends. When their respective movie shoots were over, Matt and Cameron went their separate ways—although they stayed in touch over the phone.

Cameron didn't have time for anything more than friendship in 1996, anyway. She spent most of the year on film sets: playing Heather, yet another sexy woman who comes between two brothers (Ed Burns and Mike McGlone) in *She's the One*, and Nathalie, the young "trophy wife" of actor Harvey Keitel in *Head Above Water*.

With all that going on, it took Cameron and Matt more than a year before they were in the same place long enough to begin dating. But once Matt and Cameron hooked up, they made no attempt to mask their relationship. They tried not to be concerned with what reporters might say, or where photographers might be lurking. "We don't try to hide anything," Cameron told a reporter for E! Online. "We are who we are. We're a couple. We're affectionate in a way that's comfortable for us in public. We try to live our lives the way we would if we were not famous."

By the end of 1996, Cameron's professional and personal lives were just where she wanted them to be. ShoWest, an organization of theater owners, presented her with its coveted Female Star of Tomorrow award, proving that she was on her way to Hollywood's A-list. And she and Matt were involved in a serious relationship, spending time together in both her L.A. home and his New York apartment.

For Cameron, life seemed perfect. And things were only getting sweeter.

CHAPTER 12

There's Something About Cameron

A smile that lights up a room

Cameron Diaz's smile is big and broad. It lights up a room. But there is an actress in Hollywood who is every bit as well known for her big, bright smile and infectious laugh—Julia Roberts. So imagine a comedy in which Julia and Cameron have a chance to work together. It would be a guaranteed hit—right?

That's just what the producers of *My Best Friend's Wedding* were thinking when they cast Cameron in a supporting role. *My Best Friend's Wedding* was Cameron's first big-studio picture since *The Mask*, so naturally she was a little nervous about taking on the role of Kimmy Wallace, a woman who is engaged to marry Julia Roberts's best friend.

My Best Friend's Wedding went into production in late 1996. By that time Julia Roberts was already a force to be reckoned with in Hollywood. She was one of a small handful of women who were said to be able to "open" a picture. That meant people would come to see Julia, no matter what the movie was.

Cameron was both excited and nervous to be working with Julia. She looked forward to learning from the incredibly talented actress, but she wondered how this big star would act toward her. After all, the cast (which also included Dermot Mulroney and Rupert Everett) were all going to be holed up in the same Chicago hotel during the filming.

Luckily, the cast became very close friends, and Julia even taught Cameron how to knit—the perfect hobby for an actress who has to kill time on the set between scenes.

If Cameron was afraid that the talented cast was far above her experience level, she needn't have worried. Julia had nothing but respect for Cameron as an actress and as a person. "She's very savvy," Julia told *People* magazine. "She's out there in a very open and incredibly friendly way. She's a great giggler. But at the same time she's not some giggly, perky, sophomoric blonde person."

My Best Friend's Wedding was a huge success—earning more than $120 million worldwide. The film's wide distribution brought Cameron to the attention of a whole new audience, and in 1998 she won her second major acting award—the Blockbuster Entertainment Award for Favorite Supporting Actress for her portrayal of Kimmy in *My Best Friend's Wedding*.

Cameron followed up *My Best Friend's Wedding* with a more offbeat independent film, *A Life Less Ordinary*. The film appealed to Cameron in many ways. She loved the script, and she was excited at the idea of working with the cutting-edge British actor Ewan McGregor. Most of all, she relished the opportunity to take direction from Danny Boyle, who had directed Ewan in the critically acclaimed and controversial movie, *Trainspotting*.

Unfortunately, even the combination of attractive actors, a groundbreaking script, and an innovative director cannot always guarantee a hit. In the case of *A Life Less Ordinary*, the film was a box office bomb.

Her film may have sunk, but Cameron's star was still on the rise. *Entertainment Weekly* recognized her potential, naming her the magazine's "It Girl" of 1998.

Entertainment Weekly couldn't have picked a better actress for the honor. Cameron definitely had "It"—that certain something that separates the actresses from the stars. And she was about to prove just how much "It" she had.

In October 1997, Cameron signed on to star in a comedy by Peter and Bobby Farrelly, the screenwriters-directors of the comedy smashes *Dumb & Dumber* and *Kingpin.* Peter and Bobby were thrilled to sign Cameron up to play the lead character in their new film, *There's Something About Mary.*

"Cameron is Mary," Peter told *People* magazine at the time. "Like Mary, Cameron is the ultimate woman. Every guy on the set was crazy about her."

But the only guy on the set who mattered to Cameron was Matt Dillon. Matt had signed on to play Pat Healy, a sleazy private detective who is hired to find Mary and winds up falling in love with her. For a long time, Matt and Cameron had been looking for a movie to do together. But they'd always assumed that their first joint effort would be a sweet, romantic film—not a total gross-out comedy flick like *There's Something About Mary*. But the *Mary* script totally cracked them up, and Matt decided to sign on. Besides, both Matt and Cameron knew they would have a blast making the movie. It was well known in Hollywood circles that any set that had the Farrelly brothers at the helm was primed for hijinks on- and off-camera.

Bobby and Peter were taking a big chance signing Matt and Cameron to the same film. It's not always easy being on a set in which the lead actors are romantically involved. Sometimes the actors can't separate their personal lives from the film. But by all accounts Matt and Cameron were the consummate pros on the set of *There's Something About Mary*, even though their relationship was out in the open.

"Matt would come over and rub her shoulders if it had been a long day," recalled Lin Shay, who played Mary's eccentric neighbor, in *People* magazine. "I would notice them on a bench together or stretching out with her head on his chest."

When *There's Something About Mary* opened in July 1998, nothing really happened. The Farrelly name attracted their core audience of young men, but that was hardly enough to drag it to the top of the highly competitive summer film charts. *There's Something About Mary* seemed destined to fade away, like many light comedies that come and go. But a funny thing happened on the way to Labor Day weekend. Word-of-mouth momentum started building about how outrageous and original the film was, and *There's Something About Mary* began attracting thousands of people to the theaters.

The Farrelly brothers were already known for making films with gross-out scenes in them, but they were never famous for creating romantic comedies. *There's Something About Mary* definitely had its share of disgusting jokes and over-the-top slapstick comedy, but Cameron's appearance in the film took *Mary* to another level. She was perfectly believable as a woman searching for true love. Audiences really rooted for her to discover that her perfect man had been there all the time. Because of Cameron, people who loved romance but were never before inclined to watch a Farrelly Brothers flick came to see *Mary*. And people kept on coming back to see it again and again.

The box office receipts just kept growing. *There's Something About Mary* was the little movie that could. By the time Labor Day weekend rolled around in early September, *There's Something About Mary* was the number one film in the country. Considering that Labor Day is when the studios pull out the big guns and release their best films, it was a huge accomplishment for all involved.

There's Something About Mary grossed $170 million worldwide, proving that Cameron had the star power to bring in the bucks. But more importantly it showed that Cameron was the type of actress who had the talent to carry a comedy on her shoulders. As many actors will tell you, it is tougher to do comedy than anything else. In a comedy you need a special sense of timing that not all performers are lucky enough to have.

© 1998 Steve Granitz/Retna Limited, USA

There's something about Cameron

The prestigious New York Film Critics Circle certainly took notice of Cameron's talent and timing. In 1998 they awarded her their Best Actress Award. Cameron's competition was Meryl Streep and Susan Sarandon. Both women have won plenty of awards—including Oscars. Cameron never thought she had a shot. She was totally surprised when her name appeared inside the envelope.

"This must be some sort of joke," she told *InStyle* magazine after winning the award.

But it was no joke. In fact, she also picked up the Blockbuster Entertainment Award for Favorite Actress in a Comedy that same year, for her part in *Mary*.

Unfortunately, just as her career was hitting its pinnacle, Cameron's personal life took a downswing. She and Matt split up early in 1999. Only Cameron and Matt really know what happened, but rumors had it that Matt wanted to live near his family on the East Coast, and Cameron wanted to stay close to *her* family on the West Coast.

Cameron and Matt's breakup really shouldn't have come as much of a surprise to anyone. Even when their romance was at its best, Cameron had complained to reporters, "It's hard to just pop over for the evening. We have to almost schedule meeting and just get together when we can."

Still, friends and family had hoped that if anyone could make long-distance romance work it would've been Matt and Cameron. But after a while the strain of always having to arrange to meet up in different cities got to them. Matt and Cameron made their long-distance relationship work for a long time, but they just couldn't make it to their happily-ever-after.

CHAPTER 13

A Hollywood Power Player

Cameron spent most of 1999 building on her star power. Besides being part of the amazing ensemble cast in *Being John Malkovich* (her costars included John Cusack, Catherine Keener, and of course John Malkovich), she also had a leading role in *Any Given Sunday*, which was directed by Oliver Stone.

Any Given Sunday was a big hit during the busy holiday season, and Cameron's performance as the manager of a pro football team was especially well praised. The success of *Being John Malkovich* and *Any Given Sunday*, coming right on the tail of her *Mary* success, placed Cameron in a small, elite Hollywood club of successful actresses.

After Cameron finished shooting *Any Given Sunday*, she hightailed it to Paris to begin filming an independent film called *Invisible Circus*. The role, that of a woman who commits suicide, was Cameron's most difficult to date. It was hard for the ever-positive Cameron to take on the persona of someone who finally takes the ultimate fall.

While Cameron was off filming in the City of Lights, Hollywood was all a-buzz about a new action film that was in the planning stages—a film version of *Charlie's Angels*. Drew Barrymore had already attached herself to the project, and now she and the film's other producers were looking for someone to play the other two Angels.

The role of Natalie appealed to Cameron's adventurous side. As a kid she'd watched *Charlie's Angels* and she was particularly fond of Sabrina, the brainy Angel played by Kate Jackson. Cameron thought it might be fun to sign on to the project—especially with rumors flying that some of the old Angels might come back to make cameo appearances.

Luckily, *Charlie's Angels* was a big-budget studio flick, since Cameron's new asking price was a hefty $12 million per movie. In *Charlie's Angels* Cameron earned every cent of her salary—in sweat. The *Charlie's Angels* shoot was a rigorous one, and even the super slim Cameron had to get in shape to perform some of the stunts. All those workouts were less than fun for Cameron, especially since she was not a regular at the gym.

"I've never exercised in my life," she reveals. "I can usually eat what I like and always seem to burn up energy. One day I'm just going to balloon up."

But Cameron knew all the sweat and pain was worth it. Besides, she loved working with Drew and Lucy Liu. They were an inseparable trio throughout the filming of the movie. They had a lot in common. They were all young, all successful, and all strong women.

Besides the sisterhood on the set, *Charlie's Angels* appealed to Cameron's sense of fun—and action. "I've always liked action. Now it's time to put that to the test on the screen," she says.

Before *Charlie's Angels* had even wrapped, Cameron was busy considering scripts for her next project. One in particular caught her fancy—*Success.* Cameron loved the idea of being in a film with Meryl Streep, a woman who is widely considered the greatest American actress alive today. As the summer of 2000 rolled around, Cameron and Meryl were in negotiations to do the film.

Being considered for a role in a Meryl Streep film must have felt like a dream come true for someone who only a year ago had been considered a Model-Turned-Actress. But with the success of her past films, Cameron is being offered only the cream of the crop these days. And that feels wonderful.

"As far as work goes, everything has changed," Cameron told *Premiere*. "Which is great. Who doesn't want a lot of options?"

But Cameron isn't grabbing every film she can get. She's very careful about her choices. She wants to make sure that every role she plays shows a different aspect of her personality, and that she can learn in the process. "I know it's not worth it for me to grab as much as I can. I'm just not in a race," she insists.

Cameron is obviously thrilled to be a successful working actress. But she is having difficulty adjusting to some of the newfound fame that comes with celebrity. The media spotlight that has been thrown on her is often intimidating—especially because Cameron readily admits that she "hates interviews." But she understands that part of filmmaking is publicity, and as a team player she does her best to sit for interviews despite her personal feelings about reporters and the paparazzi. "I try to keep my personal life out of it; not giving it away," she says of conversations with reporters. "I don't volunteer a lot of [personal] information."

Luckily Cameron's fans are a respectful bunch. "I'm fortunate that the people I have coming up to me are nice and want to say good things," she says. But Cameron knows just how she would get rid of someone who was less than kind to her. "I have no problem saying, 'you're a jerk, get out of my face,'" she insists.

Everything in Cameron's life is happening so fast that she sometimes regrets not having the time to sit back and enjoy it. So, she's writing all her experiences down in her journal. But we'll never find out what secrets she's scribbled down in that private book. "The last thing I want is other people reading it," she says. "What's really fun is reading your journal like a year later and realizing how much you've changed. That's the greatest thing about growing up."

Cameron knows that as one of Charlie's Angels she's become a powerful role model for young girls all over the world. And that's something she's very proud of. But don't expect Cameron to change who she is just to fulfill some ideal. "I just live my life for me," she claims.

And that life, Cameron insists, "Is all good!"

What more could an angel ask for?

© 1999 Steve Granitz/Retna Limited, USA

The face of an Angel

Cameron Quizzers

These days, Cameron Diaz is everywhere. You can find her beautiful face smiling out at you from movie posters, magazine covers, and TV talk shows. But how much do you really know about the girl behind the blue eyes? Well, here's your chance to find out. Just answer these Cameron Diaz questions. Be warned—some are really tough and not all the answers can be found in this book. Only true Cameron fans will know the answers. But if you miss one, never fear. Just turn to page 92, where all the answers appear.

1. How many weeks was *There's Something About Mary* in theaters before it hit number one on Labor Day weekend of 1998?
A. 1 B. 5 C. 7

2. Which of Cameron's relatives plays a convict in *There's Something About Mary*?

3. What was Cameron's nickname in high school?
A. Tree B. Skeletor C. Wiley

4. What did Cameron's mother give her before she left on her first overseas modeling trip?

5. How many callbacks did Cameron have to endure before she was given the role of Tina in *The Mask*?

6. True or false: Cameron competed against seventy actresses for her role in *Feeling Minnesota*.

7. Which was the first of Cameron's films to gross over $100 million?

8. True or false: Cameron's laugh actually broke the karaoke machine in *My Best Friend's Wedding*.

9. How long did Cameron and Matt Dillon know each other before they began dating?

10. Where did Cameron grow up?

11. For which agency did Cameron model?

12. Which of Cameron's parents is Cuban-American?

13. Cameron agreed to play Nathalie in *Head Above Water* because she wanted to work with which actor?
A. Ewan MacGregor B. Matt Dillon C. Harvey Keitel

14. In what city was *My Best Friend's Wedding* filmed?
A. New York B. Chicago C. Cincinnati

15. What group named Cameron its Female Star of Tomorrow in 1996?

16. What high school did Cameron graduate from?

17. In which film did Cameron play a Wall Street exec who had once been engaged to one man while having an affair with his brother?

18. What magazine named Cameron its "It Girl" of 1998?

19. True or false: Cameron drives race cars as a hobby.

20. True or false: Cameron was divorced from Matt Dillon in 1999.

Answers to the Cameron Quizzers

1. C
2. Her dad. "They were kind enough not to leave him on the cutting-room floor," she says of Peter and Bobby Farrelly.
3. B
4. A silver hairpin that could double as a weapon if she was attacked.

5. Twelve
6. True
7. *The Mask*
8. True
9. One year
10. Long Beach, California
11. Elite
12. Her dad
13. C
14. B
15. ShoWest
16. Long Beach Polytechnic High School
17. *She's the One*
18. *Entertainment Weekly*
19. True
20. False. They were never married.

Where Do You Stand?

15–20 correct: There's something about you that just screams out genius!

9–14 correct: You've obviously been spending your allowance money on movie tix— this is a great score.

5–8 correct: Yikes! Your score is slipping faster than the box office on *A Life Less Ordinary*.

0–4 correct: It's time to reread this book, and maybe stop by your local video store for a Cameron Diaz refresher course.

CHAPTER 15

Cameron's Filmography

The Mask (1994) . . . Tina Carlyle
The Last Supper (1995) . . . Jude
She's the One (1996) . . . Heather Davis
Head Above Water (1996) . . . Nathalie
Feeling Minnesota (1996) . . . Freddie
Keys to Tulsa (1997) . . . Trudy
My Best Friend's Wedding (1997) . . . Kimmy
   Wallace
A Life Less Ordinary (1997) . . . Celine
Fear and Loathing in Las Vegas (1998) . . . Blond
   TV Reporter
There's Something About Mary (1998) . . . Mary
   Jennings Matthews
Very Bad Things (1998) . . . Laura Garrety
Man Woman Film (1999) . . . Random Celebrity
Being John Malkovich (1999) . . . Lotte Schwartz
Any Given Sunday (1999) . . . Christina Pagniacci
Charlie's Angels (2000) . . . Natalie
Things You Can Tell Just by Looking at Her (2000)
   . . . Carol
Invisible Circus (2000) . . . Faith O'Connor

AFI's 100 Years, 100 Laughs: America's Funniest Movies (2000) (TV) . . . Herself
Shrek (2001) (voice) . . . The Ugly Princess
The Gangs of New York (2001) . . . Jenny

LUCY LIU

CHAPTER 16

The Girl With Something Extra

"I don't feel any different, but suddenly everyone wants to talk to me," Lucy Liu says. "I guess it comes with the territory."

Does it ever! These days, Lucy's definitely entered a new territory—super stardom. It's one thing to have a few guest-starring roles on popular TV dramas. When you're a guest star, you can still go to the supermarket or yoga class without everyone staring at you, analyzing what you're wearing, and calling the tabloids to give them false stories about you. But once you become the breakout star on a hit TV show, and have a Mel Gibson movie under your belt, there's no such thing as privacy anymore. Everyone is going to want to know what you think.

For some new stars, the constant media attention can be a problem. After all, it's hard to give an interesting interview to a reporter if you're not really that fascinating a person. Luckily, in person Lucy is as intelligent, well read, and straightforward as she is on-screen. Think about it—how many people do you know who've mastered the martial arts, taken professional photographs, and learned to play the accordion?!

Few actresses around today are able to display raw power and sex appeal simultaneously the way Lucy does. When she enters the room as Ling Woo, her character on the hit TV show *Ally McBeal*, the other actors have no choice but to pay attention to her. And neither does the television audience. Despite the fact that she's only five feet one inch, Lucy commands respect. But don't fool yourself into thinking that Lucy is as

tough and difficult as Ling is. In fact, Lucy likes to think of herself as the "anti-Ling."

"It's so much fun playing her," Lucy admits. "But I have this fear that people are going to run away

© 1999 Steve Sands/Corbis Outline

Lucy is the "anti-Ling"

from me in terror on the streets. They think I'm going to bite their heads off or something."

People run away from Lucy? No way! In fact, there's no doubt that this brainy Angel is certain to find friends and fans wherever she goes. No matter what icy, bizarre, or brave characters Lucy chooses to play, people just seem to be drawn to her natural talent and zest for life. She has genuine star quality, a rare commodity even in Hollywood.

Ironically, this was never the life Lucy had pictured for herself when she was growing up as a shy, bookish kid in Queens, New York. But life has a way of changing people's plans and taking them on a completely different journey than they've ever dreamed of.

This is the story of Lucy Liu's journey to superstardom.

CHAPTER 17

That Tough New Yorker

Lucy Alexis Liu was born on December 2, 1968. She grew up in Jackson Heights, in the Queens borough of New York City, where her parents had settled after immigrating to the United States from China.

Both of Lucy's parents were highly educated people—her mother was a biochemist and her father a civil engineer—but like many immigrants, they found it difficult to find jobs immediately in their chosen careers.

"My father was a civil engineer, . . . but at one point he ended up selling pen watches in Atlantic City," Lucy recalled to *People* magazine.

Eventually, both of Lucy's parents were able to find jobs in their professions. And while that helped the family out financially, it often left Lucy, her brother, and her sister to fend for themselves. "I was pretty much a latchkey kid," she told *People.* "I'd just come home from school and watch television until they got home."

Ironically, Lucy was not influenced by one of the hottest shows of the 1970s, *Charlie's Angels*. While other kids were desperately trying to look like the show's star, Farrah Fawcett, Lucy steered clear of the feathered-hair look. "I didn't have the flipped hair or the curves," she insists.

Although Lucy's parents were not around as much as their daughter might have hoped they would be, Lucy and her sibs never lacked for love or direction. The one thing Lucy's parents insisted upon was that their children never take for granted the amazing opportunity they had at getting a quality, free education in America. The Lius stressed to their children that being able to make money in a field that you love and being able to take care of yourself were extremely important. The result is that today, Lucy considers herself exceptionally business-oriented. That's not something many actresses can claim.

"That's a gift my dad gave me," she explains. "[It's important] to manage yourself because ultimately you're going to be by yourself in the end."

Lucy's parents' determination to make

sure that their children worked hard in school has paid off for Lucy in many ways. She likes feeling educated and in the know about many subjects. "I don't think of myself as a genius or anything, or that I have such a high IQ, but in Hollywood I feel pretty special. I feel so intelligent. People are like 'Wow! You have so much to talk about.' So it's good [that she worked so hard at her education]."

But the Liu household was not all work and no play. Lucy and her brother and sister all discovered a love of music at a very young age. "Somehow I think [my dad] was very influenced by the Osmond family," she jokes. Each child in the family played a different instrument. In Lucy's case, her father gave her a choice between playing the violin and the accordion. The accordion won.

While the Liu family music group never quite hit the pop charts the way Donny and Marie did, Lucy fell in love with the accordion. To this day she brings the giant portable keyboard on the set of *Ally McBeal* with her and plays duets with fellow accordion aficionado and costar Greg Germann during breaks.

Jackson Heights, Queens, is not exactly an area best known for its huge Asian population. In fact, when Lucy was growing up there, she was one of the few Asians in the neighborhood. Lucy says that made a big difference in the way she felt about things growing up.

"You go through a period when you don't like being Asian," she told one online magazine. "You want to be 'American.' But as I got older, I wanted to accept myself."

In high school Lucy spent every morning traveling from Jackson Heights to the more culturally diverse Manhattan. Lucy was lucky enough to have been accepted at New York City's highly acclaimed Stuyvesant High School. Unlike many of the city's local high schools, Stuyvesant is one of a few magnet schools that specialize in certain areas of study, such as math and science, fashion and design, and the performing arts. Magnet schools accept only a select group of kids from around the city. In order to get into the magnet schools, New York City high school kids have to take a test or pass an audition. As a high school specializing in math and science, Stuyvesant is one of the most difficult magnet schools to get into. Each year thousands of kids apply to Stuyvesant, but only kids who score in the top 2 percent of the test scores even have a shot at getting in. Her acceptance into

Stuyvesant is a real testament to just how intelligent Lucy Liu is.

People who went to school with Lucy during her Stuyvesant days remember her as having big hair and always dressing in black. By her own admission, Lucy says she was quiet and shy during those days. And she certainly wasn't likely to be voted "most popular" with the boys. "I was skinny with a bad haircut, which didn't amount to a very successful dating process at all," she recalls.

Still, there were some boys who were attracted to this self-proclaimed wallflower. "I had heard about French kissing but I thought it was the most disgusting thing in the world. There was one guy who was interested in me and one day he kissed me. It freaked me out so much," she recalled in *Details* magazine.

Doesn't sound like the same girl who would someday grow up to play the wild woman Ling Woo, does it?

After graduating from Stuyvesant, Lucy stayed in her native city and enrolled at New York University. Her hope was to major in Asian languages and graduate from NYU in the usual four years. But that wasn't how it happened.

"I went to NYU for a year and I was so

unhappy," she recalls. "I was living the whole alternative life, playing pool, just hanging out. So eventually I just picked up and went to the University of Michigan."

Transferring to the University of Michigan was more than just a change of scenery for Lucy. As she would soon find out, it would prove to be a major change in the whole direction of her life.

CHAPTER 18

Tumbling Down the Rabbit Hole

Moving to Ann Arbor, Michigan, was a very brave thing for Lucy to do. Not only was she moving halfway across the country, away from her family and friends, she was moving to a total college town—a major change from the big city life she was used to in New York.

Lucy viewed this adventure with characteristic daring. "I'm very independent," she explains.

Lucy found the college experience she was searching for in Ann Arbor. She jumped into life in the small college town with enthusiasm. Once

An independent woman

© 1999 Eric Charbonneau/Berliner Studio/Corbis Outline

again, she chose Asian languages as her major (today she speaks fluent Mandarin), but she also added classes in acting, dance, and voice to her roster.

During her senior year, Lucy decided to try out for a part in the university's production of Andre Gregory's adaptation of *Alice in Wonderland*. She figured that being part of a school production would be fun. But because she was not a theater major, Lucy only expected to be cast in one of the play's small supporting roles. Imagine her shock and surprise when she was cast in the lead role of Alice!

From that moment on, Lucy's dreams of being an Asian language interpreter went out the window. She knew that her passions were in the arts, and that acting would play a major role in the rest of her life.

But deciding on being a professional actress and actually getting cast in a role are two very different things. As Lucy soon learned, there are a limited number of successful actresses in the world. Most actresses spend more of their time waitressing and temping in offices than they do on the stage or screen.

After graduation, Lucy spent time in New York and California, where she began going on auditions for theater productions, commercials, and anything else she read about in the trade newspapers. But auditions don't buy food and shelter, so Lucy worked day jobs as well. "I worked seven days a week," she recalled (in a *Profile* interview) of those early days. "I used to work as a secretary during the weekdays and on weekend mornings I was an aerobics instructor. In the evenings I worked at this rib joint as a hostess because I knew I needed money if I wanted to be an actress."

Eventually, Lucy attracted the attention of an agent, and was able to get herself into more auditions. Slowly, she began to pull together an acting résumé, playing small parts and guest-starring on shows like the '80s hit drama *L.A. Law* (in which she played a foreign correspondent); *Home Improvement* (in which she played Woman #3); *NYPD Blue* (as Amy Chu, a baby-sitter); *The X-Files* (as Kim Hsin); and *Beverly Hills, 90210* (as a Peach Pit waitress named Courtney). The parts weren't huge, and they weren't going to bring Lucy stardom in the near future, but they did manage to get her some notice from casting directors.

Lucy managed to attract attention even when she *didn't* get the role. In 1990, Asian actresses from all over came to New York to audition for a part in a production of *Miss Saigon*, a musical that prominently featured Asian women. Lucy was one of the actresses who auditioned for the show. She didn't get the part, but she did get featured in an article in *The New York Times*. The article was headlined "Scores of Actors Flock to Try Out for Ethnic Roles in *Miss Saigon*."

"There aren't many Asian roles and it's very difficult to get your feet in the door," she explained in the 1990 *Times* article. "It will have so much to do with what happens in the future for us."

What Lucy really hoped was that the future would begin to hold more roles for her that were not specifically written for Asians. She wanted to be able to spread her wings and play many different types of roles.

But at the time, that seemed almost impossible. For the most part, Lucy continued to be cast in roles that were definitely intended to be played by Asians. She had parts in theater productions of *M. Butterfly*, a show that put a twist on the story of the opera *Madame Butterfly*, and in a play entitled *Fairy Bones*, in which she appeared as a young woman living in Sacramento's Chinatown.

Still, as the mid-1990s rolled around, Lucy's parts became larger. In 1994, she got cast as Mei-Sun Leow, a mother with a baby dying of AIDS, in three episodes of the nation's number one drama, *ER.*

But even as her acting dreams began to come true, Lucy was feeling incomplete as an artist. There was another side of her that needed to be fulfilled. For many years Lucy had been experimenting with photography. And, just like everything else she put her mind to, Lucy discovered that she had a real talent for that art form. On September 11, 1993, Lucy made her art gallery debut at the Cast Iron Gallery in New York's famed SoHo area. Her exhibition of photos, entitled "Unraveling," was comprised of three bodies of work. The first was a series of hand-tinted photos taken in Hong Kong. The second was a group of portraits of hands and feet, and the third was a collage in which she used photos taken at a pro-choice march in Washington.

Despite the fact that Lucy made her living professionally as an actress, she told reporters at the time that her photography was equally as important to her. "Acting and photography are both very expressive," she explained to the *Asian New Yorker.* "I don't consider myself so much as an actor or a photographer—I'm more of an artist."

But even Lucy had to admit that her acting career left her little time to take pictures, never mind put together entire exhibitions, on a regular basis. Still, Lucy seemed okay with that. As she told a reporter at the time her photo show opened, "I don't have to exhibit in a gallery every three weeks to feel engaged. I don't put myself under the gun."

It was a good thing Lucy felt that way about her dual careers. After all, she was soon to go on an audition that would change her life forever.

CHAPTER 19

Life as Ling

Having a guest-starring role on a top TV drama is a big stepping-stone in a young actress's career. Suddenly your name pops into people's heads when they are casting new shows or movies. In Lucy's case, the exposure she got on *ER* helped her land her first big-screen movie role, as a former girlfriend in the Tom Cruise flick *Jerry Maguire*. She also came to the attention of the producers of a new show called *Pearl*, which would be starring Rhea Pearlman, who was fresh off a long run as the no-nonsense waitress Carla on *Cheers*. The show also starred veteran actor Malcolm McDowell.

Because Rhea Pearlman was so well loved by the American viewing public, CBS had big hopes for *Pearl*, which told the story of a middle-aged woman who goes back to college. Lucy was extremely excited to get the role of Amy Li, a highly stressed fellow student of Pearl's.

Unfortunately, audiences weren't able to let go of Rhea's image as Carla, and the series lasted only one season. By 1997, Lucy was back pounding the pavement. She managed to score some small movie roles that year in flicks like *City of Industry*, *Flypaper*, and *Riot*. But nothing was as high-profile as her role on *Pearl*.

Then Lucy went on an audition for a role on an already established hit—*Ally McBeal*. *Ally McBeal* was the brainchild of writer-producer David E. Kelley. When the show first began in 1997, nobody expected the quirky courtroom comedy to ever be a huge success. The show had all the markings of a cult classic, though—its lead character, Ally, was an insecure lawyer who'd joined her ex-boyfriend's law firm, where his wife also worked. The firm was peppered with some strange and outrageous supporting characters.

Surprisingly, this cult classic became a national pastime. More than 18 million viewers watched the show's debut, and from then on the accolades and awards came rolling in. Before long, everybody was talking about *Ally*.

So when Lucy heard that David Kelley was looking for someone to play Nelle

Porter, the icy, beautiful, superior lawyer whom the women of *Ally McBeal* hate but the men can't take their eyes off, she was anxious to audition.

As soon as Lucy walked into the office where the auditions were being held, however, she lost all hope of ever getting the role. "There were six women there and I was the only woman of color," Lucy recalls. "And I thought, 'this is a joke. There's no way I'm getting this part.'"

As it turned out, Lucy was right. The role of Nelle went to Portia de Rossi, a tall, blond bombshell from Australia. But Lucy didn't lose the role because she was Asian; she lost the role because David Kelley saw her as "too frigid." David had planned to make Nelle more compassionate as the show went on.

"He didn't think I—me as a person—could be a friendly, warm person," Lucy explains. "I must have gone in there and been really cold, I guess."

But David Kelley couldn't seem to get Lucy out of his mind. He really wanted to find a way to use her in *Ally McBeal!*. In fact, the casting person who eventually called Lucy to tell her that she didn't get the role of Nelle mentioned to Lucy that David was planning on writing a guest-starring role just for her in the future.

But Lucy didn't believe that for a moment. "People say stuff like that all the time, especially in Hollywood," she explains. "You don't think it's actually going to happen."

Of course, in this case, it actually did. David created a calculating, lawsuit-crazy character named Ling for an episode entitled "They Eat Horses, Don't They?" In the episode, Ling hires Ally's law firm to sue a foulmouthed radio disc jockey.

The character of Ling was only supposed to be featured in one episode of *Ally McBeal*. It wasn't the permanent part Lucy had

hoped for, but playing a character written especially for her was something Lucy couldn't resist. She jumped into the role of the rich rhymes-with-witch with great excitement.

As everyone knows by now,

Everyone loves Ling!

audiences loved Ling. And before long, Lucy found herself a full-fledged member of the cast of *Ally McBeal*.

Although Ling comes across as evil (so evil that for a long time her entrances were marked with the Wicked Witch theme music from *The Wizard of Oz*), Lucy doesn't see her that way. In Lucy's eyes, her character isn't mean; she's simply misunderstood by everyone else.

Lucy compares Ling's icy coldness with that of another beloved but misunderstood TV character—Frasier's frigid wife, Lilith, on *Cheers*. "They're both originals," she explains.

Lucy says that Ling is actually a very sensitive creature. "Ling, for all her bravado, is vulnerable," she explained to Women.com. "She doesn't want to get hurt."

In her never-ending desire to keep from being hurt, Ling goes to extremes, whether it's suing practically everyone who has the bad luck of crossing her path, or eating the pet frog of one of her coworkers.

"I'm having such fun," Lucy divulged to the *Post-Gazette Magazine*. "Kelley has written some of the most interesting fun—I'm doing things that I never thought I'd be able to do. Ling brings some sort of friction and energy that's not as confused as everybody else."

One of the things Lucy loves most about playing Ling is that although Ling's love interest Richard Fish (Greg Germann) is white, there has never been a big deal made of the fact that theirs is an interracial relationship. "It's not an issue," she says.

Lucy also loves working with the *Ally McBeal* cast. Although the tight-knit group had been together for a full year before Lucy joined the show, her fellow cast members made her feel welcome from the start. "We all have such a great time working together," she assured Women.com in 1999. "I have such a difficult time keeping a straight face." In fact, Lucy admitted in one interview that

© 1999 Berliner Studio, Inc./Corbis Outline

in order to keep from laughing during her scenes with other cast members, she actually has to slap herself on the thigh—hard. That can make for some nasty black-and-blue marks.

Those bruises have

Partying with *Ally McBeal* costar Jane Krakowski

paid off. Lucy's popularity as Ling continued to grow, and by the end of the show's second season, Lucy found herself nominated for an Emmy Award in the Best Supporting Actress category. Although she didn't win the award—it went to Kirsten Johnson of *Third Rock from the Sun*—just being nominated meant that Lucy had made it to Hollywood's hot young actress list.

Playing one of the toughest women on TV could have caused a problem for Lucy. Fans often confuse actors with the characters they play. Had that happened with Ling, Lucy could have found herself being on the receiving end of some very dirty looks from *Ally McBeal* fans.

© 1999 Jeff Slocomb/Corbis Outline

Making her mom proud at the Primetime Emmy Awards

But luckily, Lucy's fans seem to be able to make the distinction—especially after meeting her.

"Actually, they're really sweet," Lucy says of her fans. "And after [we meet] they always say, 'Wow! You really are nice!' And I've thought afterwards, 'What did you expect, a Dragon lady or somebody?'"

Before long, the fan magazines caught on to what the fans had known for a while—Lucy was a versatile actress who was loaded with talent. In 1999, *People* magazine named her one of its 50 Most Beautiful People. *Entertainment Weekly* named Lucy one of the Sizzlin' Sixteen Stars of 1999. Lucy gladly accepted the kudos. But there were some honors that she gracefully felt she needed to decline.

"A lot of Asians have wanted to give me awards and come have me speak, but I turn them down," Lucy told TV Guide Online in early 1999. "Hey, give me a while. I haven't done anything to earn this yet. Don't give me an award because I'm the only person that's well known right now who's Asian."

If Lucy was looking to beef up her résumé before accepting speaking engagements, she was well on her way to doing just that. Thanks to her exposure and success on *Ally McBeal*, movie offers began rolling in. Nineteen ninety-nine was turning out to be Lucy's breakthrough year!

CHAPTER 20

Getting Payback for All the Hard Work

It was hard to miss Lucy during 1999. Not only was she a member of one of the best ensemble casts on television, she was also all over the big screen. You couldn't walk into a multiplex without seeing Lucy.

Lucy's movie roles were a diverse group. In *The Mating Habits of the Earthbound Human*, she played a slightly eccentric character called The Female's Asian Friend. That might sound like a bit part, but Lucy really had plenty of screen time. The reason the character had no name was that the film was a mockumentary—a comedic film that makes fun of documentaries. In this case it was supposed to be a documentary on human relationships. Carmen Electra was the lead actress in the movie. Her character was known simply as The Female.

Lucy had a smaller part in her next film, *True Crime*. But it was very exciting for her just the same, because the star of the movie was none other than Clint Eastwood. No matter how small your role in a Clint Eastwood film, it's a big deal just to be able to share the screen with one of Hollywood's legends. Lucy was very proud that she'd been able to get a screen credit in *True Crime*.

Lucy's next film, *Play It to the Bone*, starred two of Hollywood's big hitters—Woody Harrelson and Antonio Banderas—as aging boxers who are on their way to Las Vegas to fight each other. It's not hard to figure out why Lucy had a blast playing Lia, a woman who picks up the two men in her car, and drives them part of the way to Vegas. After all, what girl wouldn't want to be sandwiched between those two men? Not exactly a rough day at work!

But of the films Lucy appeared in during 1999, perhaps her most memorable role was as Pearl in *Payback*. *Payback* starred Mel Gibson, and naturally the producers assumed that Mel would be the major reason for the film's success. *Payback* totally played to Mel's strengths. The action-adventure showed him as a lovable bad guy. Even the movie's tag line, "Get ready to root for the bad guy," let you know that Mel was the focus of the film.

But a funny thing happened when audiences screened the movie. All eyes seemed focused on Lucy—even during the scenes she played opposite Mel. Of course, it helped that she was dressed head to toe in sexy black leather outfits, and sometimes even carried a whip. But it was Lucy's acting chops and charisma that really attracted the attention. As *Rolling Stone* put it in the magazine's review of *Payback,* "Even if she wasn't dressed in leather and cracking a whip, you'd pay heed."

After appearing in films with Mel Gibson and Clint Eastwood, casting agents suddenly began thinking of Lucy as an action kind of gal. So when Jackie Chan was looking for an actress to play the kidnapped Princess in his new action film, *Shanghai Noon,* he came straight to Lucy.

Lucy's interest in *Shanghai Noon* was motivated by more than just the chance to take on a new character on the large screen. Jackie Chan is a martial arts expert, and Lucy has been studying the martial art of Kali-Eskrima-Silat for quite a while. What is Kali-Eskrima-Silat? "Oh, you know, the knife and stick stuff," Lucy explains proudly.

Although Lucy enjoyed starring opposite

men in action flicks, there was something missing from the casts. For the most part, Lucy lacked female companionship on the set.

But that was about to change.

CHAPTER 21

An Angel Without the Wings

In 1999, young actresses all over Hollywood were tripping over each other to audition for the role of Alex in the movie version of *Charlie's Angels*. After all, once Drew and Cameron signed on, everyone in town knew that the flick had the star power to make millions—and who wouldn't want to be part of that package?

Finally, in September the film's producers announced that they had their Alex—actress Thandie Newton, who had previously starred in the Oprah Winfrey movie *Beloved*.

Thandie's casting destroyed the hopes of a lot of young Hollywood women, Lucy included. In some ways she, and the people who knew her, felt that role was made for her. After all, Alex is a smart martial arts expert who must go undercover as a model to solve a case. Sound like anyone you know?

Well, life has a way of making things work out the way you want them to. In October, Thandie Newton announced that she would no longer be available to play the role of Alex in *Charlie's Angels.* She dropped out of the film, saying that she had "scheduling conflicts," because the production schedule on her latest film, *Mission: Impossible II,* was running longer than expected.

All of which meant that there was still a shot for Lucy to get the role. She quickly put out the word that she was interested, telling the *New York Daily News* and other papers that *Charlie's Angels* was the kind of picture she was looking for.

The producers of *Charlie's Angels* were intrigued with the idea of casting Lucy in the role, but they were concerned that, like Thandie, Lucy might have a few "scheduling conflicts" of her own, since *Ally McBeal* was still in production.

And there were other problems, too. *Charlie's Angels* producer Leonard Goldberg had his eye on a big movie star, Ashley Judd, to play the role. "Ashley would be fabulous," Leonard said in an interview with the *New York Daily News.*

Unfortunately for Ashley, she couldn't play Alex because she was in bed recovering from a fractured fibula she'd injured in a jet-skiing accident.

Ashley's loss was Lucy's gain. In November 1999, Lucy finally got her wish—she was cast as Alex in *Charlie's Angels*, after weeks of negotiations to work out a schedule that would allow her to work on both the movie and *Ally McBeal*.

Being one of *Charlie's Angels* was a whole new experience for Lucy. Sure, she'd experienced the whole "star thing" by being nominated for an Emmy, and having her picture in magazines. But TV stardom is nothing like movie stardom. Now Lucy was in the big leagues—reportedly earning a seven-figure salary for her role as Alex.

One of the most exciting things to happen to Lucy was her pre-Angels appearance at the 2000 Oscars. She presented the award for Best Costume Design with Drew and Cameron. Lucy knew that as a presenter, she had to make a good showing—both onstage and on the red carpet. She had to look good, or run the risk of ridicule by Joan Rivers and other members of the "fashion police."

Luckily, when it comes to style, Lucy knows what she's doing. She wore a custom-made Versace gown with a bright sunburst design. The colorful formal made her stand out from the sea of Oscar black, and won her the applause of the fashion press. One reviewer called the dress "young and sexy at once."

Walking down the Oscar red carpet was definitely a dream come true for Lucy. Best of all, it was a dream she'd made come true with hard work and dedication to her craft. And that made the victory all the more sweet.

© 1999 Jeff Slocomb/Corbis Outline

Finally an Angel

CHAPTER 22

Learning About Lucy

Okay, so you know she plays a pretty, positive, powerhouse as Alex in *Charlie's Angels*, and that Ling is the total Miss Thing on *Ally McBeal*. But just how much do you know about the personal side of Lucy Liu? There's just one way to find out. Take this Lucy Liu quiz.

Some of the questions will be easier than winning a case on *Ally McBeal*—after all, most of the answers can be found right here in the book. But some are more difficult than choosing between Woody and Antonio in *Play It to the Bone*. Only Lucy's true fans will be able to answer those. Either way, don't worry, you'll be able to find the answers on page 131.

1. Name the first play Lucy performed in.

2. In what year was Lucy first named one of *People* magazine's 50 Most Beautiful People? A. 1998 B. 1999 C. 2000

3. Which two of these colleges did Lucy attend?
A. Yale B. New York University C. Temple University D. University of Michigan

4. On which of these TV series was Lucy a regular cast member?
A. *ER* B. *NYPD Blue* C. *Pearl*

5. What famous New York City high school did Lucy attend?

6. How tall is Lucy?

7. Which movie did Lucy describe by saying, "This movie is going to be the hugest. I mean everyone in the world is going to see it"?
A. *Star Wars Episode 1: The Phantom Menace* B. *Payback* C. *Charlie's Angels*

8. Where did Lucy's character Courtney work on *Beverly Hills, 90210*?

9. In early 2000 Lucy signed a lucrative contract to become a spokeswoman for what?

10. What did Lucy's pals have to talk her out of doing because it was too dangerous?
A. Hang gliding B. Mountain climbing
C. Buying a motorcycle

11. Which fellow *Ally McBeal* cast member does Lucy like to play accordion duets with?

12. During her short stint on *ER*, what brought Lucy's character to the hospital?

13. True or false: Because of her newfound fame, Lucy will no longer audition for roles.

14. Which New York borough did Lucy call home while growing up?
A. Queens B. Manhattan C. Staten Island

15. Who were Lucy's copresenters at the 2000 Academy Awards?

16. What kind of food did Lucy cook as a food service worker while she was waiting for her big acting break?
A. Omelettes B. Pancakes C. Sandwiches

17. Which magazine called Lucy "one of the Sizzlin' Sixteen Stars of 1999"?

18. With which *Ally McBeal* character is Ling romantically linked?

19. From what country did Lucy's parents come?

20. Which *Beloved* star did Lucy replace as Alex in *Charlie's Angels?*

Answers to Learning About Lucy

1. *Alice in Wonderland*
2. B
3. B and D

4. C
5. Stuyvesant High School
6. Five feet one inch
7. A
8. The Peach Pit restaurant
9. Revlon comestics
10. C
11. Greg Germann
12. Her baby was dying of AIDS.
13. False
14. A
15. Cameron Diaz and Drew Barrymore
16. A
17. *Entertainment Weekly*
18. Richard Fish
19. China
20. Thandie Newton

How Do You Rate?

15–20 correct: You should give Charlie a call. He could probably use a genius like you on his team of Angels.

9–14 correct: You're so in the know about Lucy. You'd never pronounce Ling with a hard g.

5–8 correct: Oops. You're score is slipping. Next week try watching *Ally McBeal,* followed by tapes of *Payback* and *Play It to the*

Bone. You need a Lucy refresher course.

0–4 correct: Are you sure you haven't been watching reruns of *I Love Lucy* instead of *Ally McBeal* on Monday nights?

Lucy's Filmography

L.A. Law (1986) (TV) . . . Foreign Correspondent
Coach (1989) (TV) . . . Nicole
Beverly Hills, 90210 (1990) (TV) . . . Courtney
Home Improvement (1991) (TV) . . . Woman #3
The X-Files (1993) (TV) . . . Kim Hsin
NYPD Blue (1993) (TV) . . . Amy Chu
ER (1994) (TV) . . . Mei Sun Low
Bang (1995) . . . Hooker
Hercules: The Legendary Journeys (1995) (TV) . . .
   Oi-Lan
Guy (1996) . . . Woman at newsstand
Jonny Quest (1996) (TV) . . . Melanie
Pearl (1996) (TV series regular) . . . Amy Li
Jerry Maguire (1996) . . . Former Girlfriend
Michael Hayes (1997) (TV) . . . Alice Woo
Flypaper (1997) . . . Dot
City of Industry (1997) . . . Cathi Rose
Riot (1997) . . . Boomer's Girlfriend
Ally McBeal (1997–present) (TV series Regular)
   . . . Ling Woo
Payback (1999) . . . Pearl

Molly (1999) . . . Brenda
True Crime (1999) . . . Toy Store Girl
Ally (1999) (TV series regular) . . . Ling Woo
The Mating Habits of the Earthbound Human
    (1999) . . . The Female's Asian Friend
Play It to the Bone (1999) . . . Lia
Shanghai Noon (2000) . . . The Princess
Charlie's Angels (2000) . . . Alex

ANGEL SITE-INGS

You don't have to call Charlie to find out what his three Angels are up to these days. The best place to keep up with the comings and goings of Drew, Cameron, and Lucy is to check out the fan Web sites that are dedicated to each of them on the Internet. The fans always seem to be the ones with the inside scoop, and the info on these sites is remarkably up to date.

But when you're surfing the net, remember to play it safe. Never give your address, phone number, or real name to *anyone* you meet over the Internet! And don't meet anyone in person who you've been introduced to over the Net. In fact, the less personal info you give your chat room buddies, the better. After all, someone who may seem like an Angel online could turn out to be quite the opposite in person.

You can find biographical info and photos of Drew, Cam, or Lucy on any of the official Web sites dedicated to their films or TV shows. But if you're looking for the 411 on Drew, Cameron, or Lucy specifically, check out the sites listed below.

FYI: Keep in mind that Web sites come

and go. By the time you call it up, one of these sites may be gone—but that's okay, because new Web sites dedicated to Drew, Cameron, and Lucy are popping up all the time.

Drew Barrymore Web Sites

Drew Barrymore—Wild Girl with a Heart of Gold
www.geocities.com/NapaValley/2508/drew.html

I Love Drew
www.trashed.org/ilovedrew/main.html

DaisyTales
www.dr3w.8m.com/

The Drew Barrymore Dominion
www.geocities.com/Hollywood/Screen/5212/index.html

Where Dreams Come Drew
www.drew-barrymore.com

Cameron Diaz Web Sites

Cameron Diaz Internet Archive
www.geocities.com/~cameron-diaz.html

Mr. Showbiz-Cameron Diaz
www.mrshowbiz.go.com/people/camerondiaz/
index.html

Best of Cameron Diaz
www.cameron-diaz.com

Great Actress-Cameron Diaz
www.great-actress.com/cameron/main.html

Cameron Diaz
www. casenet.com/people/camerondiaz.htm

Lucy Liu Web Sites

The People's Lucy Liu Website
www.canadawired.com/~katina/

Lucy Liu Page
www.deja.com/~lucyliu/

The Sizzlin' Sixteen of 1999
www.eonline.com/Features/Features/Sizzlin99/
Girls/liv3.html

THE MOVIE

Web sites are a great way to keep up with the ladies, but these days most people are interfacing with Drew, Cameron, and Lucy at the movies instead of on their computers. It seems as though everyone, everywhere, is buzzing about *Charlie's Angels.*

Drew Barrymore's insistence that the detectives use their brains instead of guns in the movie was a smart call. It changed the whole attitude of *Charlie's Angels.* Unlike the old TV show, the new movie isn't camping it up for the cameras. Instead, the film has a fresh new millennium attitude that both girls and guys can totally relate to.

That's the key to the success of *Charlie's Angels: The Movie.* There's something for everyone. It's got laughs. It's got danger. And it's got its share of romance, too.

But while the flick definitely has a strong plot (three bright detectives who save a kidnapped business exec), it's really the cast that gives the film its pizzazz. Think about it. On the male side of things you've got Bill Murray, a guy who's been cracking people up for almost thirty years (he got his big break on *Saturday Night Live* in the '70s), and

Tim Curry, a well-known character actor who is known for putting the word "bad" into bad guys. And on the female side, you have those three Angels.

Despite the fact that many women auditioned to be Charlie's Angels, now that the movie is out it's hard to imagine anyone but Drew, Cameron, and Lucy in their respective roles. They were perfectly cast as Dylan (the tough cookie), Natalie (the bookworm), and Alex (the class act). Who better to play the brilliant detectives than three strong actresses who have taken control of their own lives and careers? With all of the obstacles Drew, Cameron, and Lucy have overcome, no one could ever deny that these Angels have earned their wings.

About the Author

Nancy Krulik is the author of more than one hundred books for children and young adults. She has written biographies of many of today's major celebrities, including Leonardo DiCaprio, Ricky Martin, and 'N Sync's J. C. Chasez. She lives in Manhattan with her husband, composer Daniel Burwasser, and their two children.